private property

by Seth Kenlon

Abstract

The future, after the genetic experiments of the great Doctor Patricia R. Durham, leaves all women on the planet with snake instead of hair, and the unique and terrifying ability to blind, and kill, a man with a simple stare. The birthrate is at all-time low, the population dwindles, the world's governments are all but disbanded.

One woman walks across Amerika without a destination.

College students get drunk and cause trouble.

A man in a bar in the mid-west stops believing in love.

A radio station broadcasts old Doctor Patricia R. Durham interviews all day, every day.

An old out-of-commissioned factory crushes a tourist into an eight-inch cube of flesh and bone.

Albino cobras. Alive, and deadly. See them, five dollars per guest.

Pancakes for a dollar, a cup of coffee is seventy-five cents.

Not much has changed, really.

private property

ISBN 978-0-9847842-0-2

Chapter One

True Story: I was walking, I had been walking all day, it was a summer day.

It was a hot

summer day.

I remember exactly what I was wearing. Shorts and a t-shirt. Just trying to keep cool. This was at a time after it was dangerous for a lady to walk across the country alone. This was when it had been made safe. Because had anyone attacked me or even smiled at me, I would have burned his eyes out with my stare.

This was a Medusa Age. So I was afraid of no one.

Before women had acquired their new eyes, I would have been beaten, raped, and left for dead. My grandfather had been beaten and robbed, and this is how he died: he was bleeding from his ear, and no one would stop to help him. No one wanted blood in their cars. I wonder what they would have done if they'd known he was the greatest genetic scientist in the universe. And so he set out for the nearest hospital, and as he stumbled down a highway much as the one I am strolling along now, he began to lose his sense of balance. Eventually he fell, and he fainted in a puddle of water, and drowned. The greatest genetic scientist in the universe drowned in a puddle of muddy water no deeper than an inch and a half.

The farmer who, as he tended to the cows which he planned on slaughtering and selling as hamburgers to fast food restaurants, had watched my grandfather die later called the police. Not an ambulance but the police. Because he was upset that someone was lying on his *private property*.

Magic words.

I think of my grandfather now because of my own story. It was a hot summer day and I was tired of walking, weary from the heat. I came upon an open field, and in the field there was a tree, and so I took shelter in the shade.

My car was broken and dead two days back down the road. My knapsack was one day back. All I owned was what I wore and had in my pockets.

In the distance I could see a man approaching. I smiled. I thought "Good! some companionship at last!" I was young and naïve. This happened a few weeks ago. The man approached me and he looked down at me, my writhing hair, my glowing eyes, and with only a little fear he said: "You're on *private property*. Git off." I was amazed and appalled. I said as politely as possible that I wasn't bothering anyone and that I was *minding my own business*. He said "You're on my *private property* so yer business is my business as long as ycr here and I don't want any of it. So mind it somewhere eltse."

People can't imagine the freedom that is to be had by simple isolation. Where there are two people, there is a fifty percent chance for unresolvable conflict. These are mantras for a modern age.

My sister roped off her room into two sections: one half was for public use. The other half was *private property*, through which no one was allowed to pass. This seemed fair to me, and a good microcosmic example of sound sociological policy. Then I learned that the public half of her room was the half opposite the room's door, so that in order to reach it one would have had to pass through *private property* -- and she never permitted that.

As I continue now to walk across country, I think my sister had learned this idea from the world around her. She was not setting an example. She was imitating. My sister is dead. She is one of the ten in one-hundred females whose bodies had not been born with the new hair and eyes. So that she would not reproduce, Dr. Patricia R. Durham ended my sister's life at puberty.

> *She did not mutate properly. She's no one to blame but herself.*
> — Dr. Patricia R. Durham, speaking to my parents over the telephone of my sister

Lucky for me, I had been born a proper mutant.

I have burned out the eyes of five men and I have killed two times that number. I am one of the most attractive females I know. In fact, before I began actively burning men's eyes out, quite a few of them would watch me with great interest. Men generally don't watch women much any more. And they get frightened if a woman watches them.

Burned:

- Mr. Henry S. Johnson - Fifth grade teacher. He seemed to watch me a little too closely. I felt uncomfortable. So I burned his eyes out when at last he dared make eye contact. Possibly as a result, I failed the fifth grade that year and had to repeat it, this time with Mrs. Alice P. Fair-weather.

- Mr. Jacob G. Goodwin - A young man who whistled at me as I walked by. He never whistles at women now, because he can't see when one passes.

- Mr. Roger L. Smith - A boisterous young man who found my distress at dropping my groceries, and bending down to gather them and thereby dropping the rest of the groceries I'd been holding in my arms, sexually exciting. He and Mr. Goodwin (see above) are friends now. They walk around with their hands on one another's shoulders, tapping their red tipped canes as they go.

- Mr. Guy T. Lecher - Not his real name. I don't know his real name, so I have given him this one. He was staring at me, so I burned his eyes out. He was driving a ground-car at the time, and after the deed had been done he drove into a telephone pole. He no longer drives.

- Mr. Tom R. Harris - More of a precaution, this one. He seemed to enjoy watching me when I came into his store, so I burned out his eyes so that we could remain on good terms. I didn't want him making cat calls or to flirt. He doesn't, and we are still good friends.

I don't think he believes that I am responsible for his toasted retinas. I was with a group of my friends -- we were in the first year of high school then -- and he'd probably made eye contact with all of us in rapid succession. If he would use logic, he would realise that since I was his last sight, then I must have been the one to fry his retinas, but I think he wants to think it was someone else who did this just before he looked over to me.

Having said all of this, I find myself reminded of my one true love, Arthur P. Thomas, Jr. He was the son of the very famous business tycoon, Arthur P. Thomas, Sr. After we had made love for the first time, I burned out his eyes. I wanted his last vision to be that of me, nude and beautiful and young and in love. It is a very romantic notion and, to my knowledge, it hadn't been done before.

I do not include his name among the five men whose vision I have ended because Arthur P. Thomas, Jr. ended his life a day later. He felt I had betrayed him. He felt I did not love him.

Although he shot himself, I count him among those whom I have killed.

In truth: he is the only boy I have loved. He is the first man I killed. He is the only one I regret.

There is a barrier between men and women. Arthur P. Thomas, Jr. proved this to me. A man cannot understand the deep emotion with which a woman kills him. I imagine that Arthur P. Thomas, Jr. is sitting now in heaven, with new angelic-designed eyes, and thinks all day about how sad it was that I decided to betray him. He may not know the truth until I myself die and tell him.

Relaying messages to the dead is not possible. When someone is dead, their minds cannot be changed unless it is done by another dead person. This also means that a ghost will not listen to a message you have for someone, because their mind already does not know the message.

I know these things because Dr. Patricia R. Durham said so, and she should know; she was dead twice before.

There have been only two real friends in my life: Arthur P. Thomas, Jr. and Richard C. Brown. The latter I cared for but I did not love him. I only love Arthur P. Thomas, Jr., and this is not something I say only to sound romantic. It is the truth. I will tell you no lies. This is a decision I have made.

We were not in love, Richard C. Brown and I, but we enjoyed each other's company. At first he was afraid of girls. His father was afraid of women, too. His mother had been knocked off by Dr. Patricia R. Durham, who said dying wasn't really as bad as its reputation made it seem. In these matters I tend to trust Dr. Patricia R. Durham, but his father did not, and was afraid of even me.

Richard C. Brown, upon meeting me, averted his eyes and said Golly, you sure would make a good runner.

And so he taught me how to run and hurtle. But not once did he actually look at me. He never made eye contact. I was feeling very lonely.

After I burned out his father's brains, right through the man's eyes, Richard C. Brown started to warm up to me and even made eye contact. After that the fear was gone; we were *best friends*, and he told me that I was the only girl he liked because I was attractive and athletic. I said thank you, and shook his hand.

I think men are confused by the snakes, too. This is another barrier in proper communication. The closest thing to real intimacy that I allowed Richard C. Brown to reach was the time he asked me about my hair. There have been times of teasing, but that is not intimate. This was intimate. He was like a schoolboy when he asked, and he blushed. He asked me did I control the snakes? I said as much as possible.

It is sometimes embarrassing to have snakes for hair. When I am excited, the snakes generally make it known by twitching. When I am angry, the snakes coil and hiss. When I am relaxed, the snakes sway calmly as if lulled into hypnotism by a snake charmer. When I see someone attractive, the snakes lick their lips…

I have tried to control them. Sometimes it works. Sometimes it does not.

Richard C. Brown asked if he could touch them. I said he could. My heart was pounding in spite of myself. I did not want to fall in love again.

Know this: I did not fall in love with Richard C. Brown. But I came very close.

He stroked my hair.

A snake bit him. It was a playful, flirtatious nip. I was mortified because I did not want him to believe that this was how I thought about him.

It is a common axiom among men, which I have heard muttered recently in many roadhouses, that some women think with their hair instead of their brains.

Richard C. Brown thought the snakes had been annoyed by him. He never touched them again. I am glad, for my sake. Hopefully now he is older and more experienced and knows that when a snake bites, it is not to frighten a man away.

That is a secret I hope never gets out, for the sake of women everywhere.

Now more than ever I can understand why God in Infinite Wisdom advised the Muslims in the Eastern Cultures to cover their hair. The snakes reveal too much.

I wear sunglasses sometimes when it's dark so that my eyes do not frighten people away. Many women do now.

None now knows my name, which is why I am safe. I wonder what would occur to me if it were known that I was the grand-daughter of the late greatest genetic scientist ever. Two things seem most likely:

I would be made President of the World, or I would be killed by mobs of vengeful men and non-mutated women (if any exist).

Chapter Two

When I reached a motel, I signed the registry as "Mrs. Richard C. Brown". I signed it without thinking. Why hadn't I signed it as "Mrs. Arthur P. Thomas, Jr."? The answer is simple: he is too famous. It is common knowledge that he had taken no wife; he had died of pneumonia (suicide was considered by the family bad press) at a very young age. He had died too young to marry. He was only in high school.

My room number as #131 and this was next to a room that had been rented by a few young college students. The girls had smoked vast amounts of opium to calm their hair and glaze their eyes. The boys were very drunk. I know this because I saw them going to the ice machine.

These were ways for men and women to overcome their communication problems. They played loud music and they fucked long and noisily into the night. Someone called the police.

When I was awakened by sirens and flashing lights, I quickly put on my clothes and prepared to run. I thought someone had found out who I was, and they had come to lynch me.

Standing by the window, cold now from the night air, I watched through the curtains as the police took the boys to the police cars. They took the opium as evidence against the boys, although everyone knew boys never smoked opium. They did not arrest the girls. They did not even scold the girls.

They were afraid of the girls.

One police officer turned before closing the door, his eyes on his feet, and said: "Sorry for the trouble, ladies."

I opened my door to watch the wailing cars disappear into the sky.

I brushed back my sleeping hair and the snakes came alive. Slowly. Wearily.

I looked at my neighbour's room and saw the two college girls staring back at me. They were sad, and lonely now. I invited them in for a drink. They brought the drinks, which was lucky for me, since I had no drinks in my room. I hadn't thought of that when I'd asked them in.

The beer was German, expensive, good. I opened the curtains to watch the cars go by. They opened the beer bottles. They sat cross-legged upon the second bed, side by side. I sat by the window, in a coarse chair.

"You sure are quiet, miss."

"Say, you got a name?"

The only name I knew any more was Mrs. Richard C. Brown.

"That's no name for a lady. What's your name?"

"How did you get all the way out here? I don't see no car."

I told them that I'd walked. They did not believe me. They did not believe it was possible to reach such isolation by footpower alone, and in the heat.

They were students of a local religious school, not because they were religious but because it was the only school they had been able to get into with their poor grades. Their boy friends had enrolled because it was affordable and away from their respective parents.

They came to the motel often but no one had ever before called the police. They said they knew it wasn't the landlord because he appreciated the business.

They asked me if I'd called the police. I said I hadn't. They said if they found out I had called the police, they would beat me and rape me and leave me for dead. I said that sounded fair to me.

I had not called the police. I had been sleeping prior to the police's arrival. I told them I was a fugitive, which is not quite true, but added leverage to my defense. They believed me, since I would not, as before, tell them my name.

I only felt like a fugitive.

They told me that they were, among other things, lesbians. They told me that soon most women would be, at least on occasion. They told me that women were isolated from men now more than ever. They asked me if I was a lesbian. I said no.

They gave me a word of advice: "If you can ever get a good piece of meat, take it."

One girl fell asleep on the bed. The other told me that they were stranded now because the police had taken the car in which they had all arrived at the motel. The car had belonged to one of the boys.

She asked me why I was looking out of the window and what was there but the night sky and the highway to watch? I told her I was watching for signals from outer space.

This was a habit I'd developed with Arthur P. Thomas, Jr. So far I had not received any messages.

Then I told her an edited version of the story of my grandfather's death. I did not tell her that he was the greatest genetic scientist in the universe, which was true, but would have revealed my identity to her.

When I turned to look at her at the end of my moving tale, I saw that she, too, had fallen fast asleep.

I crawled back into my bed and slept.

Revolutionaries had been arrested not long ago on the east border of Oklahoma. They found that the world was unsatisfactory in its policies and ethics. They killed a number of policemen. The police beat and robbed them. Then they arrested them all.

Those who were expected to live were released after being charged. Those expected to perish from injuries were detained. Three days later, the newspapers reported that a prison riot had been responsible for a number of deaths. The lists of those injured on the streets and those killed in the riot were identical.

The protesters were not college students. They were middle aged men, both white-collar and blue-collar. The police raided a few nearby homes. Two non-mutated girls were found being hidden, and were arrested.

There was not often such an obvious display of protest. Most people just want to live peacefully, on their own *private property*, and to be left alone.

Not much has changed, really. Men and women still have problems communicating. People are still lonely, and they feel they are living pointless lives.

I searched for meaning once in a dream I had.

About a dead friend.

To stimulate myself at times I pour cold water over myself. It makes me jump and scream out and gasp but it awakens me and it fights the heat. The heat has always made me lethargic.

Sometimes if you stare out into the horizon at noon, you can see the air ripple and the land warp. Like a dream.

I often think it might be nice to have what people in the Sahara call a "mirage". This is an illusion that you have when you are in extreme heat. You see an island sitting pretty on a barren dune. Or a harem of girls (if you are a man) (or a lesbian college student on opium) beside cool waters, inviting you to join them.

I know this because I saw it in an old movie.

I would like to have a mirage. It would make all of this heat worth while. The sun is frying the Earth and I think we are owed something for that. The sun has not actually gotten hotter or larger. The Earth has simply become weaker. It will depress someone if they think about it too much.

> *Men Back On Top*
> — Slogan chanted by protesters in middle
> America

For fear of sounding like a revolutionary myself, I should note that I admire the protesters in middle America even though they are against my own ideals. Rather, they are against me as an ideal.

I admire the protesters because they are standing up for what they believe. They are looking for a purpose in life.

.Not much has changed.

Chapter Three

A college prank.

When I awakened, the college girls were gone. Before they had left, they had turned the bed upside-down, meaning the feet of the bed were now in the air. I did not know why they had done this. The mattress was leaning against the wall, blocking the bathroom door.

The bathroom too had been ransacked. The mirror had been covered in soap lather, the towels stuffed into the sink, and the toilet tank opened.

I splashed cold water on my face. I organised my hair, which awakened and stretched and settled. There is nothing attractive about tired hair.

The entire room had been ransacked; I noticed this after a shower. The drawers of the desk had been left open, the chair near the window moved. I had not noticed this earlier. I had been too tired.

The landlord asked Did I sleep well? I told him I had. He told me that two girls had approached him this morning. They asked him for my name. He had at first refused to give it, but they had insisted and they looked at the registry anyway.

I told him that I didn't mind.

At that point, I knew why they had ransacked my room. They were looking for identification papers. They wanted to know who I was. I assume the college girls would have sold information about me had I actually been an infamous fugitive. I am not a fugitive but if there is an edge which leads to a canyon, and the canyon is The State Of Being A Fugitive, then I am standing with my toes poetically hanging over the edge.

This is why I have forgotten my own real name.

As I have said: I have killed ten men. I know women who have killed more. none are fugitives. This is not because the law would not like to prosecute them; the law simply hasn't figured out how to do it yet.

There was a woman named Janet S. Green and she was angry at the world. And so she decided to kill people. She lived years ago, when I was just a child. She killed twenty men and boys and non-mutated women (this was before Dr. Patricia R. Durham had her way with all non-mutants). The long arm of the law tried to apprehend her but she fried the brains of the police officers. They resorted to using a hidden sharp-shooter to put an end to Janet S. Green's *reign of terror*. Her death was reported as a result of "stray gunfire", because the use of hidden sharp-shooters to put an end to a mass murderer was considered bad press. The mass murderer was entitled to a *fair trial*.

The world woke up that day. It yawned and stretched and smacked its lips and scratched its belly and took a cold shower -- and gasped and jumped. It was clear that the Medusa Age was going to change more than just a few ideas of how things should be run.

The World Almanack claims that not one female has been arrested in the past six years for even a minor offense. I believe it. Prior to that, it has been reported that only about 50,000 females had been arrested worldwide for the past five years. All for only very mild offenses -- and probably none were held for much longer than twenty-four hours.

These numbers exclude, of course, vestigial non-mutated women, who are not arrested. They are taken to Dr. Patricia R. Durham.

The world is still stretching and yawning.

The birth rate, worldwide, dropped for the first time in at least twenty years at the start of the Medusa Age.

No one is sure when "the Medusa Age" began, but by popular opinion it began with my own generation. There had been medusas before my generation, of course, but they were only the first few and changed nothing (aside from mass murderer Janet S. Green, but her death and the approximate beginning of my generation happen to coincide, and so popular opinion stands). By the time I was born, we were the new *status quo*. The old kind of woman were freaks.

As in art history

or what I know of it, anyway

the exact dates of major revolution are uncertain.

The landlord closed the registry and said he was lucky to be alive. He may have been right, although for reasons I will reveal later, he was probably wrong. But as far as he knew: if the college girls hadn't fried his brains for arguing with them then I might have, for letting the girls look at my name in the registry.

Lucky for him, the college girls liked him (this is the lesser of at least two reasons they did not kill him for protesting).

Lucky for him, I'd used a false name (this, too is the lesser of two reasons that I did not kill him. The other is: I do not kill so frivolously).

The landlord said It Just Isn't Worth It Any More. He said A Man Can't Even Make An Honest Living For Fear Of His Life. I said he was right.

The landlord said it was a Real Shame. I said he was right.

The landlord made himself a cup of coffee. He said he'd inherited the motel from his parents. He said business was slow. He said it didn't used to be like this. I said he was right.

The landlord stirred powdered cream-substitute into his coffee. He said he never bothered anyone and no one should bother him. I said he was right.

The landlord said it was strange having a motel because it wasn't *private property* and anyone could come in. He said he didn't want to die. He said if he died and became a ghost then probably he'd come to the motel and rent a room and wait for his soul to be taken into Eternal Paradise. I said he was right.

The landlord stirred five spoonfuls of sugar into his coffee. He said at least he still has coffee. He said he may not have anything else but at least he still has his morning coffee. He said did I want a cup of coffee? I said he was right. I hadn't heard a word that he'd said.

The landlord said Now I Know I Really Am Alone. I shuffled my feet and said he was right, and that time I meant it, and I left. I had all the time in the world, but not a moment to spend listening to a crazy motel landlord.

Looking back, I am not proud of this. In a way I regret this more than any man's death that I have done. I think the landlord was glad to see me go, since he'd feared for his life while I was there, but I know he could have used a friend.

To be kind to someone is not so difficult.

I do not feel that being polite is of much use to anyone. But being kind is vital.

I now know, though I did not then, that to be unkind is to kill. You are killing someone's spirit. You are killing someone from inside, and that is a terrible way to kill.

Some people,

Most

people will never be in love. They will die believing that they lived in a polite world full of insincere smiles and sweaty handshakes.

When they get to Heaven, an angel will ask the if they have left any loved ones behind. And they will say What Do You Mean "Loved Ones"?

I can picture the landlord saying this to a bewildered angel, who will then say "That Earth must be in bad shape!" because the last hundred people asked would have said the same thing -- What Do You Mean "Loved Ones"?

I prepare for this question often. Most loved ones I know have preceded me. They will be standing around in Heaven waiting to meet me. They will say they are sure glad I made it in alright. I will say I was just dying to see them all again.

I have never seen or met a woman who was not mutated properly. I do not want to. I have seen photographs of them. That is enough.

If I had been born non-mutated, I would have killed myself.

Of course, there wasn't much of a chance for that, since it was my own grandfather that created the mutation in the first place. I suspect my mother could have been the first mutated woman ever. It is a real possibility.

While I admire my grandfather for his genius, and I have always loved my mother dearly, I do not take pride in my lineage. I strive for humility in most areas of life. Just because my grandfather was a genius, it does not follow that I am. I am not.

I am just a girl walking across country.

Chapter Four

Here is another magic word: *genocide*

Examples of its use include: phrases such as:

> *That damned Dr. Durham -- it's *genocide*, what she's doing.*

And:

> *The human race is practicing *genocide* on itself because of these women.*

It is a word used only by men, who sincerely believe in it. They are mistaken, of course. I myself have known personally one woman who procreated, and I heard about another in a nearby city, which you may have heard of; it is called Philadelphia. It is famous because its name means "City of Brotherly Love", and so everyone assumes that this must mean it really is a city of brotherly love. People put a lot of faith in a name. It's just an advertisement. It's just good press. They are fooling people so people will visit the city and buy things, and give the city money.

There is a state called Florida, and that word means Land Of Flowers, or something similar to that, but the state itself is not full of flowers. It is full of big, expensive mechanical parks that no one ever goes to any more.

A man from across the ocean came into Florida searching for a fountain of youth. He didn't find it.

New human beings are born quite often.

The human race is not killing itself with mutation.

It is killing itself with unkindness.

True Story: I was sitting at a table in a café in a city. I did not know then, nor do I now, know what city I was in. I had been walking for hours that day.

I was drinking iced tea.

The glass was sweating, leaving a puddle of water upon the table.

Sometimes you feel like that puddle, if it's hot enough.

Two men approached me, and I smiled because I wanted to be friendly. I wanted to be polite. I have no desire to seem unkind.

They asked me where a local college could be found. I forget the name. I told them that I was new to the city, that I did not know where the college was.

They asked me where a main street could be found. I also have forgotten its name. I told them that I was not familiar with the city or its streets and that I did not know how they could reach that street, or even where it was.

They asked me did I know anything at all, and thanks for nothing. And they hurried away.

These were strangers to me. I had never seen them before and have not seen them since. I do not expect to. They are probably still wandering around that city, searching for their college and their main street. They are probably insulting everyone they meet, making everyone feel very poorly about them.

In a way, they are killing themselves, too.

I must look younger than I am, because I am often mistaken for a college student. I am not, and I do not plan on being a college student. I graduated from high school with only average grades because most subjects did not interest me. I do not know where my parents are now, so I have no one telling me what to do.

Once I was drinking a milkshake and I was standing at the counter and my old friend Mr. Tom R. Harris (proprietor) leaned on the counter and said "Let me ask you something, young lady."

This was after I'd burned his eyes out and he was, as I've said, oblivious to the fact that it had been me who robbed him of his sight.

I told him that I would not mind him asking a question.

He said "When you grow up"

This was when I was in high school.

"What do you want to do for a living?"

And I said What Do You Mean "Living"?

That, also, is a true story.

Mr. Tom R. Harris was a kind man, and probably he still is. I have not seen him in a very long time because I am miles and miles away from my hometown, which was a great metropolis and probably still is.

When I last saw him, Mr. Tom R. Harris believed he was on the verge of "saving the world" with milkshakes. He claimed that the Earth was too hot and that if he could initiate a programme to provide cold sodas and milkshakes to all peoples everywhere, then he would be the world's saviour.

I did not believe then that he was correct. And I do not believe now that he was correct. But he was being kind, and he was standing up for what he believed, and so I told him it was a good idea.

He also said his sight had been taken from him by God, to make him more spiritual. He felt that losing his sight separated him from the material world and lifted him to a higher spiritual plane, which he says is an invisible place which God frequents. And he says God did this.

I know for a fact that he is mistaken because, as I've said, it was I who took his sight. I did not have the heart to tell him this. Even if I had, he would have said, I suspect, that I was simply God's way of accomplishing the deed.

Which, if one considers it, is a real possibility. I have never met God, although Dr. Patricia R. Durham has met God twice, and expects to do so again soon. This has been verified by *experts in the field*. She does not claim to have conversed with God, only to have met God.

When asked by reporters what God looked like, Dr. Patricia R. Durham said "Quite like nothing I've ever seen before or even imagined." When asked by a reporter whether God was "a He or a She", Dr. Patricia R. Durham said that it was useless to use pronouns when speaking of God.

From the time her statements were published in the newspapers and magazines, it has since been impossible to find a published page which refers to God by a pronoun. The word God is a noun and a pronoun.

Dr. Patricia R. Durham has made life's great mysteries clearer for us all.

Dr. Patricia R. Durham has been to college. She is a doctor. She worked closely with my grandfather. She must be very old by now. She is said to be very ugly, which is why no one is permitted to meet with her.

Anyone who enters her office never comes back out. Because the only people who go to see Dr. Patricia R. Durham are vestigial un-mutated women, which are of no use to the human race.

Every year, two or three colleges offer Dr. Patricia R. Durham a honourary degree from their institution. Already having earned a degree, she always declines, and the college gives her one anyway, for publicity. To attract students and donations.

Chapter Five

I met the college girls again later that morning.

I was drinking coffee at a table in a diner. A waitress, who wore a uniform that was tight enough to appeal to male customers and offend prudish female customers, brought me eggs and toast.

One thing waitresses did not want to do is frighten away men. And so you find waitresses who are very attractive in restaurants, because customers who were afraid of being bitten by snakes or having their eyes burned out did not tip well.

I could be a waitress. But the job is too polite and insincere.

When I lifted my mug to drink my coffee, I became aware that two people had approached my table. The college girls sat in the bench across from me and the waitress brought them coffee. I ate. I had ordered my eggs sunny-side-up.

The waitress brought them food, took away my empty plate, re-filled my coffee. I looked out the window and drank my coffee.

I have not yet referred to these college girls by name. There is no mystery to this; I do not know their names.

The girls ate breakfast, they drank coffee. They smoked a cigarette each. They did not bother offering me one.

A jukebox was playing old rock n' roll music. New music isn't popular much any more, because no one knew what to write about. Love songs were too awkward because men and women still couldn't communicate and now rock n' roll was finally tired of pretending they could. So mostly people listen to old hollywood-jazz, and music that does not presume to be about anything.

I didn't care much for the music on the jukebox. I don't care much for music. I only like music of the Far East, because the East is where the angels are. You don't hear music like that much.

The college girls stretched and one said she had to use the restroom and that she'd be right back. The other girl asked the waitress for the cheque. Because she had no reason to believe we were separate parties. The waitress had tallied the bill on one cheque. I did not argue, and neither did the girls. They paid the bill, and I told them I had no money. They did not argue. I left a small tip. It was all I could afford.

In truth, I had money, but not much. So I did not wish to pay for breakfast if the college girls would. So I let them. I do not call this theft. I call it thrift. Without so much as bidding them adieu, I continued on my way. But the college girls followed me.

"You really aren't a fugitive after all, are youse?"

"Say, how come you're walking across country if you ain't running from something?"

I said I never claimed I wasn't running from something. I felt that this was enigmatic and poetic thing to say.

"Say, don't you ever get homesick?"

"Don't it ever get lonely, walking around alone like this?"

I said No and Sometimes.

"Golly, I sure would."

"We'll walk together, the three of us, how's about that?"

They said "Whaddya say?"

I said didn't they have to get back to college? They said It's On The Way.

"For someone our own age, you sure are strict."

"Yeah, don't you ever like to just have *fun*?"

I told them I was older than they are, and what did they call *fun*?

They said they didn't know; "Just have *fun* is all."

> *Go out to parks, and to establishments, and to*
> *one another's homes. And have fun. As fellow*
> *human beings.*
> — Dr. Patricia R. Durham, on her weekly
> radio speech

We came upon a small house, empty but for sale. They took stones from the ground and they threw the rocks at the house, shattering the windows. They kicked over the mailbox. They kicked down the For Sale sign. They broke the boards in the fence and unhinged the gate! They tore up flowers and scattered them across the yard. They sure had a lot of *fun* destroying that *private property*.

A man emerged from a nearby house. He put his hands on his hips. He said Alright Girls You've Had Your *Fun*. He told them to go back to school and leave the good folks of that town alone, and they should be ashamed of themselves, being young adults as they were.

He spoke sternly but he was careful not to threaten. He was afraid of them. And of me, too, although I did not consider myself associated with the two girls. They shouted obscenities at him and told him to go back inside and to mind his own business. He shook a fist at them and went back into his house.

He was a fat man and he'd been wearing no shirt. He had hair on his big belly and on his back and on his thick arms.

I said they'd destroyed *private property*.

They said "So what? it was *fun*!"

This senseless destruction was completely new to me. I had never seen it done before. I hadn't even imagined it was possible. To destroy *private property*, I'd assumed there had to be a reason. But they had no reason. Except *fun*.

They wouldn't have done anything to the man even if he'd chased them away. They had had their *fun*, and they wanted to be scolded.

They had taught me an important lesson. Sometimes *fun* was had just to be reprimanded. To be shown that someone was not afraid of them. This is why if you go to that motel to this day, you will find the crazy landlord still alive, still drinking his day-old coffee each morning.

It seemed strange to me.

It seemed strangely liberating to me. I wanted to break a window or kick in a fence or unhinge a gate. I want to now. But I didn't. I don't destroy anyone's *private property*. Maybe my sister's marked-off room has conditioned me.

Maybe I just don't like to have *fun*.

I hadn't really thought about *fun* until the college girls had mentioned it, and had shown me what it was. I remember only a few moments of *fun* in my life, but of a different sort. It's not their kind of *fun*.

Fun:

- Mr. Arthur P. Thomas, Jr. - I had quite a bit of *fun* with him. He used to speak at length of UFOs, which are spaceships from the other worlds, and that was *fun*. We used to spend time kissing and laughing at ourselves. That was *fun*.

- Mr. Richard C. Brown - We had *fun* of still a different sort. We enjoyed talking, and being with one another when being alone seemed less appealing. He could make a girl laugh with him and at him, and then he laughed at himself, too. When I went home at night it was with a sense that I'd brightened someone's life, and had mine brightened, too. That was *fun*, and nice to think about.

- Swimming - I discovered it was *fun* to swim in my youth, because of the heat, but after I learned that I was athletic, I swam often. I owe my current physique to my love of swimming (and running -- but this isn't as cool as swimming). It is *fun* to swim, but even more when doing this naked with a boy whom you insist you don't want to see you naked. Like with Mr. Arthur P. Thomas, Jr. early in our brief relationship, and, I confess, with Mr. Richard C. Brown throughout. I'm sure I tortured that poor boy. But probably he enjoyed it.

- Driving - Sitting behind a steering lever, passing fields and cities at phenomenal speed is *fun*. I know from experience, and now that I have no car, I miss it even more.

There may have been other occurrences of *fun* in my life. *Fun* may be transient in nature, so that what was considered *fun* many years ago no longer seems *fun* later. In this way, you feel you've had less *fun* than you actually have.

It is theoretically possible

that I have had a life filled with *fun* even to the point of being indulgent, but I am not aware of it now because I no longer see *fun* as I may have in youth. I asked the college girls were they sure that had been *fun*?

They said it had been "a blast."

They asked what I thought was *fun*. I told them swimming was *fun*. And so was driving. Because I did not want to discuss my personal life with them. I made no mention of my long lost Mr. Arthur P. Thomas, Jr. or my old friend Mr. Richard C. Brown.

They must have been reading my mind about those two boys, because they said I was lucky to be married. They thought I was married. Because I'd signed the motel registry as Mrs. Richard C. Brown.

They said most boys were afraid of them. They were afraid of having their eyes burned out, and of marrying someone with snakes on her head. They said boys got drunk and took them to motels, but that never lasted long.

Chapter Six

When we walked by a cemetery, the girls became melancholy.

We saw many graves, and they were marked "Mother" or "Wife" or "Daughter" and sometimes all three. We could almost see the souls of these vestigial women wandering through the graveyard, their hair blowing in the wind, and their eyes black and shallow. Not like us, with our eyes glowing and our hair writhing, unaffected by the breeze.

One girl lit a cigarette. The other kicked at the grass. I read a tombstone.

> *In Rejection Of The New Order*
> — Actual Tombstone Inscription

This was grossly inaccurate. Although I did not know the "beloved mother" who lay six feet under our feet, I knew enough to not believe the inscription. I will reveal how I know the inscription was pure fantasy: There is no New Order.

The noble vestigial female who was being munched up by beetles and worms under our feet had not died in rejection of a New World Order. A New Order has not been established; no one would even claim that this was an intention. She had died, I suspect, at Dr. Patricia R. Durham's skilled hands -- because this "beloved mother" was not needed by the human race.

Imagine this "beloved mother" alive to-day. She would be giving birth to more females like herself. They would all be harassed, and molested, and raped, and beaten, and left for dead.

The very idea makes me sad.

The college girls are younger and not as intelligent as I am. They think the women before us had simple and beautiful lives.

I think now that some spirits may have been whispering dirty lies into their ears.

"That was a time when a woman could be a woman, and a man could be a man."

"I'll bet people back then had a lot of *fun*."

"They used to get married right away, and they had kids, and built houses, and they had *private property* where they raised their family."

"They just don't make us like they used to."

I said you could never go home again. But they didn't know what that meant, which was alright, because I had only said it to sound sympathetic even though I was not, because I have no false romanticism about those women.

The girls sat down on a mausoleum and smoked and wept. I picked apart a flower I'd found near a tombstone. Someone had dropped it and left it.

I said He Loves Me, He Loves Me Not. This is a poem I learned in my youth. When I learned it, I did not know what it meant. Now I say it as a tribute to Mr. Arthur P. Thomas, Jr., who no doubt still feels love for me, but also does not allow himself to love me since he still believes that I betrayed him.

One girl said "I just don't know."

"I have a lot of problems. I need help. I'm trying, but I have a lot of problems."

I picked apart the flower, reciting my poem.

"It's all fucked up. I don't even have anyone I can talk to, except you."

"These souls frighten me away."

I am sure the spirits had been bothering those college girls. I told them we should go. I told them we didn't have all day, but we did. I told them I was in a hurry, but I wasn't. I told them they had to get back to school, but I didn't really care.

The last petal I pulled from the flower was He Loves Me Not. This is how I know Mr. Arthur P. Thomas, Jr.'s ghost has not yet been told of my true motivation for taking his sight, and my love for him. Unless he thinks to ask a passing angel, or God, he will probably not be told until I myself am six feet under.

I asked the college girls did they believe in God?

They said "Yeah, I guess."

I said when they died what did they think their souls would do?

They said wander around the gravcyard and whisper into the ears of people passing by.

They said they hoped they didn't die soon.

They also mentioned that they hated life.

They said what was it like to be married? They still believed, and probably still do to this day, that I was married. I had not, and have not, given them any reason to believe otherwise.

I told them I didn't know, because at the time I had forgotten about my new false name.

"Don't you live with your husband?"

"You should know what it's like to be married, seeing as you've got a husband and all."

"You got any kids?"

"Say, how about a house? You got one of them?"

We had left the cemetery, and they were cheerful again. They were happy to be not-dead.

I told them marriage was not *fun*. Because I didn't want to make them sad about being not-married.

I told them I didn't have a house or any children -- both of which are true statements. Marriage, of course, I cannot honestly comment on either way. For all I know, it could be as *fun* as swimming, or as morose as a cemetery. You can't be sure, I suspect, until you've tried it.

Marriages are still very common. It isn't as if there's a New World Order that has abolished marriage. I know one person who got married recently, and my parents were married, and I knew of a few other people who were married. Dr. Patricia R. Durham says that if we give it one more generation, then we will see even more marriages.

I believe she is correct.

I myself would have been married, I think, if it hadn't been for romance, and the lack of proper communication. And still I could be married if I want to be, but I do not love the boy who I know would marry me if given the chance. I do not know why.

Sometimes, when I am walking alone or sitting in a field and I am feeling lonely, I think I should start loving someone else, and forget about Mr. Arthur P. Thomas, Jr. If Mr. Richard C. Brown were around at those times, I guess I might be married now.

But he isn't, and I'm not. I am probably about four years older than the college girls. I have not been to college but am smarter than them both. That says something about college, I think.

It was hot.

It was after noon but the sun was still high, and the Earth is very weak. Dr. Patricia R. Durham, who is older than any of us, believes in a few generations we will all have darker skin to fight the sun. This is within her field of study, so I will not be surprised if she's the very genius to make sure that this very thing happens. Maybe soon I will be vestigial, and only dark skinned people will be needed. Soon we will all be African, and safe.

I am darker than I used to be. Because I have been walking across country, and the sun has darkened my skin. I think pale skin is ugly, and I hope it is eliminated next. There is too much pink and not enough brown on my body. This cannot be changed.

Chapter Seven

There was a lake behind the cemetery, and it was shaded by trees. So we stopped at the lake and undressed and jumped into the cool water.

The college girls were pale and out of shape. They smoked and drank too much, and stayed indoors. I swam like a fish. They waded like hippopotami. I waded like a flamingo. They swam like ducks. I splashed water at them. They screamed and splashed water back at me, but I was on the other side of the lake by then.

Mr. Richard C. Brown undressed behind bushes, and then ran, and jumped in. He was safe, but I'd caught a glimpse of him when he ran. I'm sure he knew that. I undressed behind a tree and slipped into the lake quietly, secretly. I swam up behind him, and put my knees on his waist, and he was frightened by even this small amount of contact, and struggled and swam away. I have an evil laugh, and it excited him to hear it.

I tortured him. I do not know why. I guess it was *fun*.

A trick I had was to splash him with water. I would move my hands, raised my body for momentum, and splash. But his eyes were wide open because when I raised my body, he would see my bare breasts. My splash stung his eyes and he would be embarrassed for letting his guard down, and he would not be able to see straight for the next half hour.

The water was cool. I swam underwater, like a mermaid.

It invigorated me. It revitalised my hair, and it writhed happily like water snakes. I came to rest upon a tree's root, it was underwater, in the bank. I watched clouds pass over the tree branches. The college girls had started to swim. Slowly, unsure of themselves. They were enjoying it, though.

To frighten Mr. Richard C. Brown, I would disappear underwater. He was afraid I would castrate him. This is what Dr. Sigmund Freud says. All men and boys were afraid of this. I would stay underwater and he did not know where I was or what I was planning. He would swim to the edge of the lake and jump out onto shore. Then I would lift my head and laugh at him because he was naked, and he would jump back in with a splash to punish me.

Obviously these were the games of two very curious people. To my knowledge, Mr. Richard C. Brown never saw me naked, but I certainly tried. I let him see most of me at some point, but never all of me all at once.

Dressing by the lake, I slipped into a shirt. I jumped out and sat on the shore, my legs carefully crossed.

I could feel Mr. Richard C. Brown's eyes on my legs, in the vestigial hair between them. I scolded him and he jumped out to dress himself. To this day, I wonder whether he too felt my eyes upon him when he did this.

Any other man would have gotten his eyes burned out for looking at me as Mr. Richard C. Brown looked at me when we swam together. It excited me to have him look at me. I hope I did not drive Mr. Richard C. Brown out of his mind.

I watched the clouds, and I saw one that looked like Mr. Richard Brown. The college girls swam over to where I sat. They found footing. They stood before me.

"Whatcha thinkin' about?"

"Yeah, you sure look dreamy."

I pointed to the cloud and told them that was how my "husband" looked.

"But that's a car!"

"No, it's a violin!"

I told them there was no Right or Wrong where clouds were concerned.

"Suppose you tell us how you got so tan."

"And how do stay so thin?"

I told them I've been walking across country in the sun, and I was an athlete. They touched my waist and asked what my secret was. I said don't drink beer often, and do one-hundred sit-ups each night before bed. They said they liked beer, and doing sit-ups was too much work.

The girls sprawled out on the grass to get a tan. They weren't thinking straight. They would not tan in the shade of so many trees.

They wanted me to look at them. They wanted to feel Eyes upon their bodies. I looked at them but I was not impressed.

Mr. Richard C. Brown would have been impressed by the girls. He was at that age, when I knew him. Probably now he has learned to be afraid of women. But I hope not. I hope he is married, and has had children with dark skin, and is happy. I hope when he looks up at clouds, he sees only cars and violins.

Those are simple things to see in clouds. You should never see faces in clouds, or places you have left, or things you meant to do but never got the chance.

That is all I see in clouds, lately.

I have felt pressure on me to find someone in life who I could claim. Someone I know will not leave or change. This is what people fear: opening their eyes and seeing that everything is different. They cannot read because the letters have changed. They cannot speak because the language has changed. They cannot smile because the world is unfamiliar. They cannot cry out because all of the people are strangers.

I do not know for sure that I will ever open my eyes and see that everything has changed. But when I am lonely, that is how I feel. I feel that everything is different.

And I feel no one knows me, and to be completely unknown is upsetting.

It is like being a ghost.

Chapter Eight

I have met a ghost.

A scream in the night, a broken window -- sounds of civilisation. Armies, politics, cars, clothes, drinks, tv shows, colleges, best seller lists, absurdities of zoo life.

It is clear

that people have no idea

as to what they want.

Regardless of how they act, what they tell themselves and each other -- they do not know.

Lives are like, and always have been, uncompleted sentences. Fragments in the middle of a busy paragraph.

The ghost I had met told me of a sort of parody with a predictable name.

Life, Death, Haunting.

Ghosts generally claim to have been close to anyone and everyone they meet. This is a post-mortem psychosis. Every face is a familiar one. I had denied ever having known him. This was true: I sincerely had no recollection of ever having seen him before.

I stumbled as I walked and a stranger passing by asked if anything was the matter? and Are You A-O.K.?

I thought she was a ghost and said I don't know you! I've never known you! and hurried on down the street and the stranger grinned her bewildered grin and pushed back her hat and said Well Gee Whiz!

Home was like a closet

cluttered

a space for storing useless items which I could not recall how I'd ever come to own. But I could not bring myself to throw them out. People used to scold me about this. Coats and dresses sometimes hung from the ceiling, like a closet, where the pipes were.

In my youth, I could look at someone and if they were not aware of my glance, I could read their mind.

Once I saw a crazy person on a bench in a park and he was chirping like a bird. I caught a secret glance at a stranger, smiling at the crazy person, and read her mind: the stranger was thinking "How can that crazy bum chirp like that and not feel... crazy?"

I caught a man stealing a second glance at a girl in a tight bright pink shirt. He was thinking a common enough thought.

Simple and concise.

"Nice shirt."

A man on the subway stared at his knees. I watched him for a long time and his thoughts came through clearly because he was not aware that he was being watched by me. He was staring at his knees. He was like a statue. He was thinking: "Why am I doing this again?"

My home, when I lived there, was small and empty in its neat clutter. It may still be, only it is no longer my home. There was at one point the question of honesty in one's own life, and this had destroyed my faith in my possessions.

Simple things made me laugh then.

A scruffy dog once bit a grumpy neighbour's shoe. So I laughed. A young boy uncomfortable with life once said something silly. So I laughed to make him smile. I could not laugh at tv stars or business people or politicians any more. I had even found it difficult to react to a pay cheque, when I had a job. I have no job now. How can I? I am hiking across country.

Before I knew Arthur P. Thomas, Jr., I once spent two months avoiding an uninteresting boy in high school who found me charming. Boys weren't like men; they didn't care that girls had eyes that could kill. They were still too curious about girls to care. When he sent me flowers, I accepted his dinner invitation.

This was clear: I had no idea what I wanted.

Quite often I would turn on loud music. I would find after the first song that I was tired of it.

Once a night, or every other night, I would pick up my telephone and I would dial a number.

My one and only friend's telephone number.

Because my friend, a Mr. Richard C. Brown, was home reading or sleeping.

I would dial the number just to hear a friendly voice say "Hello?"

Ashamed or nervous for having called again I would sit silently

on the floor,

perspiration on my forehead and in my palms.

I would stutter and stammer in an effort to respond. I was young.

The familiar friendly voice said again -- "Hello??"

I croaked and sighed and laughed uneasily but I found no words. So I hung up, each time. So he wouldn't read my thoughts over the telephone lines.

I learned later that he thought such calls were an epidemic, happening to everyone, because when he brought them up in conversation the next day at school, I always told him that the same thing happened to me.

My friend Mr. Richard C. Brown was intelligent. But he was far too trusting.

To sell one's own convictions is forbidden among the dignified elite. But to forsake them for love is considered a noble sacrifice. This has always been true, and maybe it will always be this way.

When I find myself speaking to someone, silently asking them to smile or to shake my hand, I can feel myself forsaking them.

Like having a cigarette after having given up smoking.

At home I was safe

      because at home I was alone

And alone is the way to be when one is a ghost, so when I was home I was a ghost, claiming to know everyone I met.

Chapter Nine

Dr. Sigmund Freud was a genius in his own time, but knew nothing about our time. He could not have known that women would soon have snakes for hair and eyes that could blind or even kill. Dr. Sigmund Freud was not a fortune teller. He was just a man who was afraid of being castrated.

I can say honestly that if I were given the chance, I would not castrate, or cause the castration of, a man. If a man offended or threatened me, I would kill him, but I would not remove a body part. If I were in love with a man, I would have no reason to castrate him, so he would have nothing to fear.

Given this information, it may seem that Dr. Sigmund Freud was not such a genius after all. However, just because women have no desire to castrate men, it does not follow that men don't fear castration.

> *It must be remembered that men and women do not communicate well.*
> — Dr. Patricia R. Durham, in a radio
> interview

It is true. Men and women do not communicate well. Let there be no doubt of this fact. Because most of the time they don't even know what they themselves want, much less what one another wants.

Consider, for example, me and Mr. Richard C. Brown swimming in the lake, naked but hiding from one another. At the same time, we gave one another glimpses of what we were otherwise hiding.

We should have either been rolling in the grass fucking like beasts in the springtime or we should not have been there at all. But we were there, and not once did we so much as kiss.

When my true love Mr. Arthur P. Thomas, Jr. and I had swam together, we played the same games (how else would I have thought to play this game with poor, innocent Mr. Richard C. Brown?) and we never kissed each other, because we knew what one kiss would have led to. And we were young and not ready to make love.

The decision to make love had been a complicated one, and well planned. A neighbour was going out of town on business. I was to water her plants once a day. Mr. Arthur P. Thomas, Jr. and I planned also on making love in their bed on a Friday night, after watering the plants for that day.

This was planned out a month in advance. We prepared through a series of carefully encoded notes exchanged in math class. I started taking something called The Pill, which is medicine to prevent procreation.

Needless to say, The Pill is becoming very hard to find lately. People like to procreate more than ever. Because the chance to procreate just doesn't present itself as often as it used to.

I do not know why people like to procreate. It may give them the feeling that they are helping the human race.

Or it may be something they do when they feel their relationship has become stagnate, and that it can no longer evolve on its own. So they make it develop mutually by looking after a child.

Or it may be a purely instinctual desire, with no logic behind it. Much like falling in love. We may never know.

I asked the college girls if they had any steady boyfriends.

"No boy wants to go steady with a girl any more."

"Wasn't it that way before you were married?"

I told them it was, mostly, but if a girl tried, she could find long-term relationships. They said I was one in a million. They may have been right, but I don't think so.

I told them when Dr. Sigmund Freud was alive, men were afraid of being castrated. Now men just fear being blinded, or killed. It is the same basic problem of communication.

They asked what castration was. I told them. no one thinks much about castration now, because no one wants to castrate anyone. Rapists were castrated once, long ago. Now they are blinded, or killed, more often.

I asked the college girls if they would castrate someone. They laughed and said they did not understand why they would ever imagine castrating someone. I said what about a rapist? They said they would just kill anyone who tried to rape them, and blind anyone who thought about it.

It was exactly what I'd expected them to say. It is what I said. It is what any woman would say.

Killed:

- Mr. Dean Q. Johnson - A young man who decided that he would attempt to beat and rape me, when I was in high school. He had a very long stick, and he hit me with this, and then held it between his legs and told me that I would never see a larger penis nor have a larger one inside me. Those were his last words. I learned his name by reading the following day's obituaries. He was my very first murder, and I felt very proud of myself for being so quick to act. I was only sorry that he'd been able to hit me at all, but he'd done so from behind, so it wasn't my fault.

- Mr. Robert D. Kemp - A neighbour. For killing him, my parents grounded me for a week. I was not allowed to go out with friends. They did not believe that I'd killed him for a good reason, although I did. I did not like Mr. Kemp ever, because he was grumpy, and cruel to his pets. Admittedly, I probably should have only blinded him when I saw that he was watching me undress through a window. And probably I shouldn't have left my window open as I undressed. But I was so upset that I killed him. But I was young, and being punished by my parents taught me a valuable lesson.

There have been many other men who have perished because of my glance. Perhaps I will list more later. These two were my first victims. Note that neither were castrated.

Communication, after centuries of development, still is surprisingly inadequate.

I started humming a tune. I do not know what the tune was.

"What's that you're humming?"

They were sitting up now. I told them I did not know and that I had made it up. They said I was a creative person to be able to make up tunes to hum. They said it sounded nice.

They were correct to say that I am creative. I have always been a creative person, for as long as I can remember. As a child I drew pictures with crayons and with no skill. But I felt a desire for skill. Children have poor motor skills. They have no coordination. I never developed enough coordination in my hand to draw well with crayons, or anything else for that matter.

But I am creative now in other ways.

My own physical appearance is a testament to my eye for beauty.

I am also a writer.

As a child, and into my more recent years, I read books as often as I could. It was the only subject that interested me in school. I read less now because I own no books. As I have said, all that I own is on my person.

I have written ten novels, only the last three of which are worth reading. The earlier ones are not well written. They were written when I was young.

I am currently writing my memoirs. These will be true stories of my life. I will be frank and honest in my memoirs.

The most recent three books I have written are fiction. One is a romantic tale about a dwarf who falls in love in the moonlight with a faerie, and all day he searches to find the faerie again, but cannot find her. That night, the dwarf has a dream about the faerie. The next day he searches for her with even greater resolve. He stops sleeping because his dreams torture him with visions of his beloved faerie. Day and night, he searches for that faerie. At the end of the book, the dwarf dies from lack of sleep, never having seen the faerie again.

It's a story about desiring what you cannot achieve or obtain. Many people go through life pursuing goals they will never reach.

Maybe you have already begun to suspect the reason. The dwarf never actually saw a faerie; he only dreamt that he'd met a faerie. The faerie had been a dream all along. But he is just a character in a book and so he doesn't think of this, and he continues to search for the faerie, and that causes his eventual demise. In a twist of fate, the only way he can actually see the faerie again (by sleeping) is seen as torment, and so he avoids it, and that is how he dies.

The tragedy, of course, is that I know many people who are just as oblivious. And they really don't have any excuse. Their goals are pure fantasy, like the faerie, but they go on trying to make them real.

I dressed, and so did the college girls. We'd had enough swimming. I knew in a few hours I would wish I hadn't left. But at that time, I felt I'd had enough. The problem with lakes is that you can't take them with you. When I got hot later, I would have no lake to swim in. I would just have to bear it.

The college girls said they couldn't wait to get back to school now. They said they would spend the night in front of a fan. They would drink lemonade. They would chomp on ice, and put ice on their shoulders, and let it melt.

They said they sure were eager to get back to school.

They said that they would take a cold shower together, and then they would make love, because they didn't care who fucked them, just as long as they fucked. I don't know if they are really lesbians. I think they were just young, and upset. I was, too. I am still. But at least I had memories of Mr. Arthur P. Thomas, Jr. And at least I'd been able to tease Mr. Richard C. Brown.

These college girls sure liked boys. So do I. But I hadn't met one interesting in a long time.

On the way, the college girls stopped at a convenience store and bought a bottle of beer each. They offered me one, but I took water instead. Not many people know that beer helps dehydrate you. There isn't anything quite like water.

The human body consists largely of water. Why we do not evaporate into a human steam cloud, I do not know.

Then again, It Ain't Over Til It's Over. This is a saying popular now. Someone famous probably said it, and ever since then we all say it. Many things I hear myself uttering turn out to be repetitious of someone famous, whether I was aware of it or not.

If I were world-famous, I would say things that made no sense whatsoever and then watch as people tried to work these phrases into their every day conversation.

If it weren't for Dr. Patricia R. Durham's unequaled wisdom, famous people could easily be eliminated with complete disregard. Of course, in this case, there would be a large segment of the world's population that would have nothing to say.

The girls drank their beer and quoted its slogan, written on the label.

Have Beer, Have *Fun*
— Beer slogan, paraphrased

My water had no slogan on its label. If it did, it probably would have been:

Drink Water, Don't Become A Steam Cloud

Chapter Ten

I have yet to meet an intelligent college student. They speak in a jargon they have learned in college so that they sound intelligent, but they rarely say much more than ad slogans and quotes from famous people.

I am sometimes told

that I often contradict

myself.

And I am asked Why?

For instance, I have said that I greatly admire Dr. Patricia R. Durham. Everyone does. And as everyone knows, Dr. Patricia R. Durham went to college. Yct I've just said that I have never met an intelligent college student. Aside from minor technicalities -- such as the fact that she is not a college student but a graduate -- this is clearly a contradiction.

Lucky for me, I am not bothered by contradictions. I believe, and have believed for many years, that contradictions are what personality is based on. Consistency does not exist in the human mind for long. A person who enjoys being a bachelor later gets married. Someone who does not believe in God prays in an emergency. A boy who fears girls buys a friend flowers. A person who buys only American cars falls in love with a German car and ends up buying it.

I have never met anyone who is actually consistent. I myself am not consistent, nor do I need to be. I have stopped trying.

I still sometimes make attempts at understanding myself. So far I have had no real success. I have created many theories about my behaviour and my feelings, but by the very next week I have proved the theories wrong.

My mind wandered, and I thought about winning a million dollars, which is done with great frequency in a very famous western town called Las Vegas. If I had won a million dollars, I would buy a home by the ocean, alone, and live there with memories. Until finally someone walked by, and then we would become friends. Assuming this person is a beach bum and has no money, I would use my money to build a house for this person. And we would be happy, in our community of two. We would not bother each other too often, but often enough so that neither of us went insane from loneliness.

This person doesn't have to be a man. I have no illusions about men walking into my life and making it worth living. These stories were once called faerie Tales but they have been forgotten now. no one believes in them.

Faerie Tales used to be a sort of unconscious religion among people, long before I was born. Women of the time, who were often raped and beaten and left for dead, believed that men were princes and had to buy them food and had to support them, whether or not she worked for a living herself. Men believed that women were mysterious wanderers who regularly bewitched men into being slaves.

This is what I am now: a mysterious wanderer. But one thing I've never done is that I've never bewitched a man into being my slave. I wouldn't know how to. And I wouldn't want to.

The beach bum could be a man. Or a woman or a sea goddess or even a talking sea turtle for all I care. It doesn't matter that much to me.

Since it won't ever happen, I guess it really doesn't matter.

I asked the college girls what would they do if they won a million dollars each. They said they would leave college, go to Europe, travel, and later settle down on the Italian Riviera.

This was not a bad idea. And surprisingly similar to mine.

I said I guessed there just wasn't that much to do with a million dollars. Or with life. You travel, you have a little *fun* -- you publish your books -- and then you *settle down* to live in peaceful boredom.

A more technical term for Peaceful Boredom is: "Lethargy". I strive for Lethargy often. It is why, I imagine, the college girls think I don't know how to have *fun*. When they finished their beer, they threw the bottles at trees, and watched them shatter into small pieces. They said it was *fun*.

We reached a busy road, but no one would stop to give us a ride. The men motorists were afraid of strange women, and the women motorists just didn't care to stop. People don't often stop their cars for much at all. I didn't, when I had a car. Driving was just too much *fun* to stop.

If I won a million dollars, a car would not be on my shopping list. I have learned to live without one, and now cars seem almost vulgar to me. They seem to have minds of their own. As if the cars are driving the people at The Wheel and not the other way around.

I've personally witnessed the transformation of usually very kind people when they get behind The Wheel. They start the car, and curse at anything that gets in their way. And they hit the dashboard when a car in front of them is going too slow, and drive close to the bumper to urge them to go faster, and then rush around them, and speed up again until the other car is out of sight. They yell out of the window at faster cars. They run through red lights. They drive on the curb.

These cars are taking over. People just don't know it yet. They think they are driving because the car goes in the direction that they turn The Wheel. But I wonder if they ever suspect that the car is the one turning The Wheel, and their hands along with it.

I think I should write a congressman about this and I would, if I believed in politicians. But I haven't seen the News lately, and I wonder if congressmen even exist any more.

The cars passed by so quickly that for a moment I imagined there were no congressmen left and there were no laws and no speed limits. I was on the verge of panic when at last I realised I had no proof that that all had fallen apart, and no reason to panic if it had.

The girls hiked up their skirts and put out their thumbs but still no one bothered to stop. They didn't even slow down. It was just a law of luck that when one wants to attract attention, everyone ignores them.

As for myself: I did not want a ride. I was content to walk. I was walking across country. I had fallen into a habit. Once I'd reached the coast, I would have to find a different habit. But for now I was walking across country. I sensed civilisation was near. This is not a sixth sense that I have. It is just deduction. We were on a busy road, and most of the cars were driving in one direction, toward the horizon before us; west. It was the way we were traveling. It was the way to civilisation.

The college girls said we were getting near their college. They said it was always busy near their college. Students came and went. Trucks delivered unhealthy food so the students could spend too much money on getting fat. Parents came to the college to scold their spoiled children, and then they drove away feeling helpless and depressed.

The human race is alive and kicking.

Chapter Eleven

The college was small. It was surrounded by a small city. It was a religious institution. Its students and the city were not.

People waved when the college girls passed. Friends from college. Girls, mostly. They smoked and drank and spoke loudly and laughed at me because I was a stranger. The college girls did not apologise. I did not mind. I ignored them. There was a guardhouse at the entrance of the college, but there was no guard. We walked right in.

It would have been silly to have a man guarding the college, because he would have been afraid of any woman who asked to be let into the campus. And no woman wants a job as a guard because it is a job that would rely on her burning eyes -- and to take a job with this solitary qualification is to say that you are a freak.

At least, that is how everyone looks at it.

So now if ever I hear myself saying that I wish I had a job, I remind myself that I could have easily taken a job guarding a college, so I've no one to blame but myself.

I don't imagine anyone cares to invade the college. no one is in the mood for that sort of *fun* any more. What would they do once they were inside? They could destroy some *private property* but then all of the students would probably end up tearing them limb from limb. So the guardhouse remains empty, the gates always opened, and the college safe.

The college was quiet and lonely. I wondered where all of the students were. The college girls said everyone was out having *fun* that night. They were all painting the town red. The college girls said they were lucky. They said they were the smart ones. They would stay in to-night and cool off. It would be a peaceful night, since everyone was away.

They invited me to their dormitory for drinks. I said it was getting late and that I should depart to find food and lodging. They said I could have just one drink, so I agreed, in hopes of them falling asleep, in which case I would be able to spend the night in their dorm room. When they awoke in the morning, I would say I had fallen asleep by accident, just as they had. It was my plan.

This was my plan but it did not work. I was not allowed into their dormitory at all. I got no further than the lobby. Here is a true story about what happened:

A student, mean and ugly and probably an over-achiever, told us it was after visiting hours. No guests were allowed inside the dormitory this late on a school night. She was the dorm chaperone. It was her job, placed upon her in exchange for free lodging during her tenure at the institution. She asked where they had been and she said she hadn't seen them come back last night.

I theorise that she was an over-achiever because her inquiries went beyond what I thought her duties probably were as dorm-leader.

She said "Keep your drugs and sex outside of this dormitory. It's not allowed here."

She said "You probably missed all of your classes to-day."

She also said "I wonder what your parents would say if they knew you spent all of your money on drugs. And on sex."

She made notes in a black notebook. She implied it was about their behaviour.

The college girls said I was a friend of theirs and they only wanted to show me their dormitory room.

She said "No visitors after hours. This is *private property*."

She said "I would advise you to keep that in mind."

She waved her finger at me and stomped her foot and breathed out heavily and put her hands on her waist. She said she *knew my type*.

I don't think I ever bid the college girls good-bye but I did leave the college campus, and the dorm-leader said she bet I was going away to find drugs and sex, and opened her books and resumed her studying. She said final exams were only months away and there is *No Time Like The Present*.

Of this, at least, we can all be sure: There really is no time like the present. The dorm-leader says so.

Chapter Twelve

Probably it would be physically possible for me to go into any motel and stand before the landlord and demand free boarding for the night in exchange for his vision, or his life. This option has always been open to any able bodied human being. But it does not happen often. It did not happen all of the time in the past. People just don't do it.

And if they did, then while they slept in their free-of-cost bed, they had their throats slit by a very annoyed landlord with a master key and a courtesy razor.

Now you understand why finding lodging was a very real problem for me in my travels. Lodging cost money, and I was trying to be frugal. Traveling, even on foot, is an expensive venture.

A room in an all-night porn-film theatre, with benches, was empty. So I slept. Bad music from cheap films lulled me to sleep.

Many years ago the theatre had clearly been a popular family destination. The room in which I slept was a waiting area. People had to wait for one audience to leave the theatre before they could go in. Now people don't have to wait. They walk in and out of the movies whenever they wanted to, because these weren't the sorts of films you had to see from beginning to end. You just went in to see people fuck, and when you'd seen enough, you left. Probably the theatre could have kept the same movie playing over and over again and no one would have noticed.

Men, women, and children had to wait years ago. They waited eagerly to see an entertaining film together. They would hold hands. They would skip into the theatre and take seats, and then fall asleep. Now only men go into the theatre, and all it plays is pornography. They don't fall asleep anymore, because they are very interested in what is happening on screen.

Once a man fell asleep in his bathtub while soaking in hot water and soap. I read about it. He drowned. A distant relative of an old friend of mine fell asleep while driving a car. Now he's a ghost on the highway, and so is the family into whom his car drove. Probably they are very upset with him for turning them into ghosts on a highway, but no amount of complaining can really change that now. Remember that ghosts can learn nothing new from people who are alive, so it would be useless to explain this to them.

In spite of these extreme examples, sleeping is not always dangerous. But there is much risk in sleeping, and probably there always will be. Even if we all had eyes in the back of our head, it would be a risk, because those eyes would have to sleep, too.

That is one development in the human race that I hope does not happen: eyes in the back of the head. Although it is a popular saying, I do not believe anyone would actually want to have eyes in the back of their head.

But if they did, probably my grandfather could have found a way to give it to them. If only he hadn't fallen asleep in a puddle of muddy water an inch and a half deep.

I do not miss my grandfather on a personal level, because I have almost no memory of him. But I miss his genius, and I am sorry that the world cannot benefit further from it.

A number of men passed by my little lobby that night but not one stopped to tell me to leave because I was on *private property*. They just did not care. And not one stopped to look at me or to touch me or to kiss me. Because they just did not care to have their eyes burned out.

At midnight it became too noisy to sleep any longer. Three women and one man were fucking in a variety of different combinations, and they were making so much noise that I could hear them all the way in the lobby, and I could not sleep. A saxophone was playing in the background.

They sure were having a lot of *fun*.

I do not know if people in porn movies are actually having sexual intercourse. It does not sound like it.

I have never seen a pornographic movie because I have no interest in them. But I have heard many of them, all during that one night I spent in the lobby of the porn theatre.

There is not that much to hear, really.

I left the theatre because I was sure I'd get no more sleep that night. Not until later, when I was tired enough to sleep through bad saxophone music and bad acting. A man in a wide hat saw me leaving the theatre and looked away but he said "Having a little *fun* to-night, are we?"

I ignored him.

Although I do not have eyes in the back of my head, I could feel his gaze on my legs. I was wearing shorts. He was watching my legs with great interest.

I did not burn his eyes out, for this reason: he had no way of knowing that I would sense his eyes upon me. He had looked away from me until I had passed him.

You cannot control who looks at you or what they think about you. I think it is wrong for a man to stare lustfully at a woman when she is obviously aware of it. I would not stare at a man who was aware of me; this would make him feel uncomfortable.

So I did not acknowledge the man in the wide hat because as far as he knew, he was stealing a glance as politely as possible.

I think now, looking back at it., that the man thought I had been watching the movies in the theatre. And that is why he said "Having a little *fun* to-night, are we?"

I cannot be sure, and I will never know for sure, but I think he was trying to be friendly. Maybe he owned the theatre. Maybe he was a frequent guest of the theatre, and he was happy to have found someone who appreciated the films as much as he did. Maybe he was a famous movie critic, coming to see a little porn to analyse a genre. Or maybe he was just a lonely man who liked to go to porn movies.

When he spoke to me, he was smoking a cigarette. His voice sounded like the gravel under my feet on a highway. He said "You're one in a million."

I imagine this man went home that night believing he had seen an apparition or a ghost from the past. He probably thought that I was the last person on Earth having *fun*. He probably thought I was not even real, since I was having fun. I imagine I turned his life around. He probably gave up smoking that night, and gave up porn, too, and climbed a mountain to find a wiseman to learn how to have the same kind of *fun* I was having. The poor man doesn't realise, even to this day, I imagine, that I wasn't having *fun* that night. I was just trying to get a little sleep, and bad acting and bad music was keeping me awake.

Chapter Thirteen

Being, as I was, very tired yet very restless because I'd been awakened, I went to find something to drink. I wanted to relax. I wanted to find some place peaceful.

The little city was not peaceful. It had too much money to make, and too much *private property* to pay for.

I heard someone once say that if everyone worked an equal amount, then the world would have a much more balanced society, and no one would really be poor because anything they could possibly want would be easily achieved because everyone in the world would be working at it. They also mentioned that there would be far less work to be done per person, so great is the potential work force.

The problem, they say, is that many people on Earth don't work, and many who do are engaged in useless activities only called work. Politicians are a good example, although I admit that I'm not positive they still exist. Accountants are another good example. If everyone worked, accountants wouldn't be stuck behind their desks any more because they'd be working instead, and besides, they wouldn't have any money to keep track of because people wouldn't need money like they do now. There would be such an abundance of food and manufactured goods that money really would be silly. It would be what was called long ago "a moot point".

I have found in my own personal experience that money does not satisfy. The more someone gains, the more one wants. This is not a new concept, but it is true.

People know when to stop eating because their stomach starts to hurt after a while. But money is painless. Imagine someone whose stomach could not hurt sitting in front of an endless buffet of chocolates. I imagine they would be dead within a day.

Chocolate is a dangerous substance and can actually lead to death. Some people are allergic to it, so they die when they eat it. Dogs die if you feed them chocolate. Some people are addicted to chocolate, and they grow fat on it, and their arteries become congested, and their hearts wear out. In the newspaper, such deaths are called "Natural Causes".

The newspaper has not yet decided on how to list a death caused by having one's brains fried. A few were listed as murders, but now they are usually listed as Hemorrhaging or Inflammation Of Vital Tissues, both of which are inaccurate. The newspaper feels it is more professional to be inaccurate with complicated phrases than it is to be accurate with a phrase like "He died because he was lecherous, so he had his brain toasted."

I found a soda joint that was open, and I went in and I went to the counter. It reminded me of my old high school hang out, run by my old friend Mr. Tom R. Harris whose eyes I did burn out as a precaution, and who is probably still on what he believes is a divine mission to save the world with milkshakes. The soda joint wasn't really similar to my high school hang out, but it had been so long since I'd been in one that I couldn't help but think fondly of my old friend Mr. Tom R. Harris.

The soda jerk behind the counter uttered this universal question: "What'll it be?"

He said: "What can I do you for?"

He said: "Swell evenin'."

I took a seat on a stool at the counter and ordered a malt.

     a chocolate malt.

I was tired but could not sleep. I felt a chocolate malt would relax me. It would make me feel less tired and more at peace, and then maybe I'd be able to relax and drift sweetly into sleep.

The soda jerk was talking but I didn't listen. I hadn't even been aware he was talking at first. He was chattering. He was talking about the night, about the students around town and their behaviour, about college, about malts, about working late hours, about the sorts of customers he gets, about anything that came to his restless mind. He was a college student, and a klutz. He dropped everything he touched. First the malt cup, then a spoon, then the mixing blade, and even the chocolate mixture itself just before he put it under the mixer. Each time he went on as if nothing had happened; he got a new cup, a new spoon, a new mixing blade, and after he'd served me he started cleaning. He was still talking. He hadn't stopped talking.

He kept a mop close at hand, and he started cleaning the first malt that he'd spilled onto the floor. He cleaned automatically, like it was a part of the process of making a malt. Maybe the person who had trained him for the job had spilled malt once, and he now spilled malt each time because he thought it was part of the job.

He was a college student. I know because he told me. Three times. He had a beard, and he thought it made him look older, and more responsible. He was working at the soda fountain to pay for college. He had applied for money from the government but they wanted him to join the military and allow them to shave his head, his beard, and brainwash him. He'd declined, so they gave him no money. Now he worked nights as a soda jerk, days as a grocer, and he attended classes in the time left over.

He asked me what I thought of that. I told him that he was a real pot walloper.

He said he did not mind his hectic schedule because he found his job as a soda jerk so easy that he never minded being at work. The other job he hated.

I must have been listening after all.

He said he was a passivist.

He said even if he saw a cockroach, the most repulsive creature on the face of this planet, he would not kill it.

I said even if he saw one crawling around in the soda fountain? Even if one was crawling over a customer's ice cream?

He said even then, he would not kill the little wretch.

I said didn't they carry germs?

He said "So do we. So do we."

I was by that time convinced that my attendant was insane. He was detached from reality. I also decided I did not want to pay for my chocolate malt, because it wasn't worth the money, and I couldn't help but wonder if any cockroaches had previously inhabited my cup.

I asked him what he would do if I walked out of the soda joint without paying, and would he call the police?

He said he wouldn't really do anything, and besides the police never come when called.

Generally speaking, there really is usually some sort of penalty imposed when someone decides not to pay for goods delivered to and accepted by them. How else can one expect to make customers pay? I asked the soda jerk how he usually enforced the rule that customers must pay for their meals or drinks.

He said the owner and day manager keeps a shot gun behind the counter, and isn't afraid of anyone. He said his own personal policy, of which the day manager was unaware, was based on something he called *the honour system*, which assumes that customers will pay because they feel it is the right thing to do.

I suspect that the soda jerk doesn't do much for the establishment's income. It should be clear by now, I think, that I had encountered a genuinely insane person who was just barely functional in society.

I do not necessarily believe in Insanity as opposed to Normalcy. I recognise, and I did even then, that everyone on the entire planet Earth could possibly be insane as a general rule, but that one form of delusion is more prevalent than others and so is established as the Norm. Every form of insanity outside of this category is called Insane.

So this young man was insane in a way that was not socially accepted, but he was clearly healthy enough to work and to attend college classes. Whether his strange delusions will hinder him from operating in society later on in life cannot be predicted.

My own view of the world and life and purpose is not healthy, and this is why I admit that it is very possible that the entire populous of the Earth is insane, myself included. But I would never establish a soda fountain on The Honour System, and if I ever see a cockroach, I will kill it until its body is smeared across the ground and I would post signs over its remains in whatever language cockroaches speak to serve as a warning to them. I am being hyperbolic, of course.

It has been a constant surprise to me that cockroaches still exist as a race. Humankind has committed innumerable atrocities throughout its history, from killing Indians and Jews and Africans, to driving the dodo bird completely into extinction, and killing most of the whales and making certain species extinct, and ruining forests, and nearly ruining the very atmosphere which we breathe, and littering oceans. I feel very strongly that if they turned their imaginative destructiveness to cockroaches, the species would vanish from the world within a few years.

There is nothing that the human race could not destroy. When they destroy something, they know they control it, and then usually once it is gone they are sad and they miss it.

The one thing they can't destroy were Indians and Jews and Africans. They certainly tried, though.

The human race, try as they might, cannot seem to destroy themselves.

They do not, then, control themselves.

It is simple logic.

Nor do they have any firm idea as to what they want. All of this may not be literal insanity by clinical definitions, but it does sound like it to many people, myself included.

That is why I admit that the soda jerk may not have been alone in his insanity in general terms, but I argue that clearly he was insane in a different manner than the rest of the world. The soda jerk said he was majoring in social work. He said he wanted to make the world a better place for children and for poor people.

This is a very common notion in people. None can say whether it is responsible for what may be a universal insanity, or whether the insanity is responsible for the almost universal notion. The soda jerk was taking classes on sociology, using a new text book with chapters on the newest, most exciting social troubles.

Outside of the soda joint I could hear music in the street. A crowd was leaving a nightclub and laughing. They were all having *fun*.

The *fun* would not stop until dawn came. This is what the soda jerk told me. He said they were having Good Clean *Fun* and it was better this than fighting and rioting.

I longed to move on in my journey. The city was too busy for me. I felt as if the music and *fun* and laughter were closing in on me, demanding I leave its *private property*.

I paid for my chocolate malt and left the soda fountain. I would await the dawn in silence if I could find it. I would not find it, but I did not know this at the time. I would try three places of refuge before the night was over; and after that the dawn would arrive at last.

Chapter Fourteen

Three is a magic number. It has been this way since the beginning of time. You may ask anyone, and they will tell you so.

The first place of sanctuary that I tried was a diner, but truckers were there, and they were loud and rude and boisterous.

The second place I tried was a church, but its doors were locked. A sign on the door explained; people too often strolled in and stole things. Candlesticks, crosses, goblets, icons.

People broke into a church.

That is a temple of God.

This is why God in Infinite Wisdom commanded in the East that thieves have their hands cut off. After stealing twice, one can't steal any more. Unless one takes things with one's teeth, but then one risks having one's head cut off.

The Eastern world is very different. If I were ever elected president, I would instate laws to Easternise the nation, and I would also make other improvements in the social structure which are too numerous to mention.

The third place I tried was an alley but there was a man and a woman there, and the woman was giving him head. He was berating her verbally. He was enjoying the experience. He was a paying customer, and she aimed to please.

By the time I'd tried the alley, the sky was gray. When I left, the sky was blue. And orange. The sun was rising. The sun was big business. It was on television. It was in books and in the newspaper. Everyone hated the sun and liked to read about why they hated it. It was too hot.

Of course, the sun hadn't gotten any hotter. The planet Earth had gotten weaker. It was being baked. And you can't turn it off. This is why dark skin will be the next important standard for human beings. Cold blood may be useful, too, but that may be too complicated. Maybe that would be too complicated even for my grandfather, were he alive.

The first time I realised I saw my grandfather's name in public was when I saw it written as graffiti on a bathroom wall, and that's when I knew I had the potential of becoming very infamous. I know my grandfather must have been a great man to have done what he has done. I have very little memory of him, though. I suspect I met the great Dr. Patricia R. Durham in my youth, since she worked so closely with my grandfather, but it would have been when I was only a child, and I don't remember.

Since that time I first saw my grandfather's name on the bathroom stall, I have seen it many other times in similar situations. And then I became aware that his name was also on the television and in the newspaper. It still would be, if the world hadn't instead turned its attention from my grandfather to his resourceful assistant, the great Dr. Patricia R. Durham.

> *As everyone knows by now, no one really knows anything.*
> — Dr. Patricia R. Durham, in a radio speech

She said it in a speech once. I read it in a book.

Some people like to say that when she began weeding out all of the non-mutated women, she also made sure that every record of her own existence was destroyed. Some people say she is paranoid. I don't think either is true. It is true that it's very difficult to find much in libraries on Dr. Patricia R. Durham, but that does not mean she had it all destroyed.

If I ever heard anyone say these things about Dr. Patricia R. Durham, I would burn out their eyes or report them to The Authorities. If there still is such a thing as The Authorities.

People have faith that The Authorities exist, although I don't know many people who claim to have met them. I think the problem is semantics. The Authorities used to mean things like police and judges and courts and governments. But now it also means people associated with Dr. Patricia R. Durham. I believe in her Authorities, but I don't believe in the other kind because lately I haven't seen any evidence that it exists. People are the local authorities, mostly. Men shoot guns at criminals, and women toast the retinas of potential rapists.

If I were president, I would resign, and move the capitol to the opposite coast, to where Dr. Patricia R. Durham lives.

I have no desire to have authority or responsibility. I would much rather live a simple and peaceful life somewhere away from the Maddening Crowd. A house on the coast. I would want to live on the coast and watch the sun rise each morning and set each evening. I would awaken early enough to see the sun rise. I would have my breakfast outside in the cool morning air just after daybreak. If ever I got too tired, I would just take a nap during the day, and no one would be around to keep me awake.

Authority is so offensive to so many people because it assumes that your desires are less important than those of the authorities's. People only like authority when their desires happen to be the same as the authorities's. So a man might really like the idea of policemen who carry around big guns and shoot people, until that man tries to shoot his wife, at which point his desire is counter to the desires of the police, and so the police shoot his knee caps off, kick him around a little, and toss him unceremoniously into a jail cell. Then the man is no longer fond of police authority. It happens all of the time.

But I doubt that any central authority still exists. Individual parts of what used to be a government probably function out of habit, but probably if anyone actually thought to try to call the President, a pre-recorded message would say that the number was out of service, and to hang up and try your call again.

No one does anything about this because, I think, no one really knows what they want to have done about it. I don't think anything should be done. I can't remember when the last election was held. I don't vote, but I think I would have heard about an election if there had been one. I like it with no authority. Walking across country makes me feel about as free as I've ever felt in my entire life.

In a society of many people, it is important that individuals come to an understanding about what sorts of behaviour will be acceptable. And what will not be tolerated. These are common limits. They are the measure of freedom in a society.

They are decided upon through mutual agreement.

Needless to say: the wider the margin between what is acceptable and what is unacceptable, the greater the freedom. It only makes sense. So it could be said that the people who control what is accepted are exactly the same people who define freedom.

I hope this is understood, because it is an important point.

It's generally acknowledged by pretty much everyone that there has to be some limits to what individuals may do in the company of others. no one wants someone to be so free that they can just go around and attack people, and beat them, and rape them, and leave them for dead. So arguments do not tend to get started over what limits have been put on a society. People usually argue about who gets to decide on them.

People will argue about what the limits are, but not as much as they argue about who is making up the limits. Because a lot of people want a few limits here and there. I don't. But a lot of people do.

A lot of countries have spent a lot of time and effort experimenting with different types of governments. And by now most people are beginning to suspect, I think, that the ones deciding on how human freedom is going to be limited has not been the common people themselves. It never has been. It's been the ruling classes placed above them all along. And I think people have started to feel like they had the wool pulled over their eyes.

A lot of people will say that the decisions made by whatever body of people ruling the mass public always reflect the desires and wishes of those people. I read a book as a girl, and the ruling class in the book was a servant class to the people. They were paid in peanuts, which is just an expression, meaning They Were Not Paid Well. Kings and Queens live in castles, and Presidents live in mansions. The rulers in that old book I read were given almost no luxuries. There is a big difference there.

The Constitution of the United States of America is a very famous document and always has been. Most people consider it sort of sacred. If you say anything bad about the Constitution, they will say that you are an Anarchist or a Communist or a Traitor, and no one will talk to you. I did this once, and no one talked to me for the rest of the day. But they all talked about me, and nothing kind was said. I was upset then, but not now. And I won't be again.

The Constitution starts off saying that it was written by the people, which simply is not true, and with a lie is a bad way to start off.

Governments now are supposed to be models of a larger environment. This is what everyone claims. They put a hundred men in a room and say that whatever happens in that room is the same thing that happens outside of the room, so the laws they make must be pretty good. They call these men in the room a Parliament or a Senate. no one is too sure, I suspect, if they even bother to do it any more. I personally doubt it.

Governments say that they do this because they can't figure out a way of counting everyone's opinion when a population is counted by the millions. And believe it or not, no one in hundreds of years of Parliaments and Senates ever thought to ask why the governments found it so easy to go around and collect taxes from millions of people, yet they are unable to count votes from the same millions of people. If you did not pay taxes, you were usually thrown into jail. They were that accurate when they are collecting taxes. But when it comes to counting votes, they just generalised by way of a Senate, or a Parliament. You would think someone would have asked this important question at some point during the past few centuries, but no one happened to think of it, I guess.

And a method for people to elect a representative was established.

And a method for the representatives to make laws was established.

But a method for the people to express their opinions on the laws that the representatives made was never established. People just voted for a general political tendency, and then they just hoped that their Elected Representative will be consistent in those tendencies when making up new laws.

It sounds difficult to believe, but this is precisely how people lived for hundreds of years. And they still do, presumably, except that I haven't really heard much about the government lately, or elections, or votes. A big problem was when people started to see that the Ruling Class that was making all the laws wasn't just made up of the people they thought they voted for. People like to vote for Presidents and Senators, and they make a lot of money when they win. And people think they've really done something when they vote to make someone rich.

Of course, governments like the Constitution is supposed to be about, don't really exist. They can't exist, because a government consisting of people would be anarchy, and anarchy can't have a Constitution and Ruling Class.

Most people I have met think Anarchy is the same thing as Chaos, because they can't imagine people being responsible enough not to kill one another like madwomen and madmen.

A Ruling Class consists, in actuality, not only of elected officials who are not effectively communicating with the public, but also of the society's rich upper class. The businesspeople. And people like that. Like movie stars, if they exist any more. And lawyers, if there are courts any more.

The two sometimes overlap, but it isn't necessary for a person in the upper class to be elected just to have power in politics. Money is power, and power is money. Power is also sex, but this is a slightly different matter. Power is a lot of things, but money is the one that applies best here.

Chapter Fifteen

I know power is money. And I know all of the tricks, too, although I myself am not rich at all. There are loopholes that let rich people stay rich. One way is for a rich person to "give" his wife a gift of many thousands of dollars, and since it was a gift, that money cannot be taxed by the government. The loophole, of course, is that the wife has the money now, and she will just give it right back to him, one way or another.

If the rich people have children, they can give these gifts to their children's bank account, too.

It is legal. You can ask a lawyer. She will tell you.

Politics is a game for the rich. They like to see which rich businessman can earn whatever title he is running for that election year. Women could play, too, but no one liked them. Of course I don't know if anyone plays this game any more. But it was big business at one point, and it was not taken lightly. There were media events built around these contests, and the media attracted lots of ads, and the ads attracted the paying public. There were weekly magazines that sustained themselves on political speculation, political debate, and then political elections, and then it started all over again. It was good entertainment for the middle classes of a country. Celebrities went out of style, but politics was exciting all of the time. The poor people were too busy trying to survive to be entertained with it.

I am not entertained by much, either. I am poor, but I am not struggling to survive. No more than anyone else, any way.

Without the ruling class, I guess there wouldn't be any limits on freedom, and no one would complain about it. People would just have to limit themselves. I consider myself very free walking across the country, and I don't think anyone is limiting me. I am limiting myself. I could rob people, and blind anyone I wanted, but I don't. I wouldn't want to, either. I'm just a walking, talking, breathing example of anarchy. It's not so bad. So I don't mind if someone calls me an anarchist.

If I ever happen to be in capitol city of this fine land, maybe I will go to the White House, just to check to see if anyone is living there. If not, and if the White House is on the beach, maybe I will move in. I imagine people who hadn't heard that there was no government any more would be pretty surprised to see me answer the door when they came around to visit.

I have never been to the capitol. I only know it is a white house in a district called Columbia, which is either in Virginia or Maryland. Maryland is the only state in the nation that claims Catholicism as its official religion.

Catholics sprung from an empire long ago. It was the Roman Empire, hence the full name of the religion itself is Roman Catholicism. Which actually means Universal Roman, if you translate it literally. Actually it translates loosely to the Universal Roman Church, because one of the Roman Emperors declared Christianity as the official religion of the empire, and that is how it became so popular. A similar thing happened for Islam when the Byzantine Empire expanded across Eastern Europe and Northern Africa.

There is a pope who lives in Rome, and he is leader of the Catholic Church. They worship God, and Jesus Of Nazareth, and an intangible spirit for which no one really has a name. They just call it a holy spirit. They are quite fond of the virginal Mary Of Nazareth. She was a jewish woman who gave birth to Jesus Of Nazareth, and since he is an embodiment of God, she in a sense actually gave birth to God. You can't make this sort of thing up.

God was a good friend, a few hundred years later, with a man named Muhammad, who conversed with an angel named Gabriel (who in fact was also friends with Mary Of Nazareth, and that seems a little too significant to be coincidence, to me. These are major religions, and there seems to be a common cast sometimes), and wrote a book, and traveled to Mecca and built a Kabbah, which Gabriel and his friends could use as a sort of landing pod.

If I could visit any place in the world, I would visit the Kabbah.

There are places on the planet which are cosmic phone booths. The Kabbah is one of the most important ones. The city of Jerusalem is another important one. There is a place called Stonehenge on an island, and that is another. Also a place called Delphi, which was once a great temple, but is now a place to go for bargain gift shoppes. But it is still an important place.

Many people used to fear police states and other forms of tyranny, even religious ones. But none of this has come to pass after all. Now it's the individualist's state, in which everyone is their own government and cold war. There is probably anarchy in a sense but there is not chaos. Because no one wants to start a war with someone else, unless they are sure they would win. Then it is over quickly and it's not really a war at all; just Natural Selection, more or less.

Jesus Of Nazareth was politically submissive. He was a jewish man living in a Roman Empire. He told his friends to pay Roman taxes without complaints. Muhammad started a form of politics based on the religion he was also starting. He called this government an Ummah, and he called his religion Islam.

Now I don't think there really is such a thing as politics or religion. Just a lot of people, and they are their own Ummah.

On my journey across the country, I once saw a rich person, and he had a nice car and nice clothes and I don't think he knew the government had evaporated. I don't know that the government itself knows it has evaporated. But looking around me as I walked across the country, I would say that everyone else knows it.

Something happened to me when I read a book called The Republic, which was written by a man named Plato, as it is often translated, although that's not how it looks to me in Greek. My Greek isn't great, but I know when I see the word PAATUN it doesn't say Plato.

What happened was that I was sick for a day.

Just from reading that book.

I was OK until Book Twenty-Nine, and after that I got sick, and was sick for the rest of the day.

I remember it had been a peaceful, gentle day, with no reason to become sick. I read the book while lying on the grass and also in a hammock, I was sitting in the shade of two trees.

If word got out that Plato had been making fun of this nation since even before Jesus Christ was born, much less this nation, there might be a revolution. This was how I learned democracy didn't work. As I read the book, I saw words

Magic words

Private words

that were supposed to have been the sole invention of the first Americans, those men with their heads on the money. But Plato knew them already, and he knew about the real estate racket, and about interest rates on loans, and he even knew about the suffragettes.

How could Plato have known about the suffragettes? It is clear why I became sick. I could not believe what I was reading. I have learned that money is very important, but it is not, really. And that is something a society ruled by the rich must never learn if they are to take their rulers seriously.

I learned it. And I don't take the government seriously. Plato really did a lot for my perception of the country, and the world, even. If ever I meet Plato, I would like to tell him this, and have him autograph a copy of his book for me. Except that if ever I met Plato, I would be dead, because Plato is about as dead as they get, considering how long he's been dead for.

When I learn something is true, but I cannot believe it, I have the tendency to become physically ill until I am able to accept it.

Chapter Sixteen

If people believe in you, then you can invent your own dignity. Or, sometimes, if you are convincing enough, you may invent your own dignity so that people will believe you.

I once knew a man who told a group of Italians that he too was italian, and they all at once looked at him as a brother. Fraternity. But I had just heard him a week ago telling a group of Greeks that he was Greek, and a week before that he had claimed to be of German descent. He was also a military veteran, a firefighter, a police officer veteran, and ay other thing he needed to be. He invented his own dignity. And people believed in him, too, and so he could tell them anything he wanted, and they would not question him, and so he could never let them down. As long as they believed.

It was a comfortable way to be, I imagine.

"If I had a million dollars, I would be happy" is a common thing to hear out on the streets. But it is not true. If I personally had a million dollars then I would have all the material items I desire. That is true. But it is not true for everyone. Some people have a million dollars. Some people have more. And they still work, they still buy things, and they still want more. And if you borrowed money from them, they would still charge interest until you paid it all back, and they would still get upset if you couldn't pay rent on time, and they will be upset if your car breaks down on the road and holds them up in traffic because they will say that *time is money*. And they do believe it.

Time, of course, has nothing to do with money.

This must seem strange coming from someone who has never worked. But remember that I have very little money. I am not rich. I have had a lot of time, though. So if *time is money* then I should be rich.

When I left the little college town it was awakening from its long sleepless night, and people were opening up their stores and cooking breakfast and delivering the newspaper. The college was coming to life, too, and all of the good students who hadn't gotten drunk last night were now hurrying sleepily to their expensive classes so they could spend an hour transcribing and memorising every bad joke and every estimated fact that their professor regurgitated from his textbooks. They were paying to be allowed to do this.

I wasn't hungry yet, so I skipped breakfast. It was tempting to eat regardlessly, because there was a small restaurant that advertised pancakes for a dollar. If ever you are in whatever town that was, and happen to see a brick building advertising pancakes for a dollar, that is probably the restaurant I saw. If you are not in a hurry, you may want to stop in for some of those Silver Dollar Pancakes because breakfast for a dollar is hard to beat these days.

The following portion of my journey was very pleasant. I made many mental notes on this portion, as if I was a travel guide, and so I will make suggestions of places to visit when in the area.

I got pancakes later on. But not until that evening. For most of the day I just ate fruit I took off of trees along the road.

I don't know what state I was in at first, nor what road I was following, but it was a dirt road. I was in the Mid-West, which is unofficially sort of an independent nation all its own. Some people there care for nothing but *private property* and will literally shoot anyone who is on it without permission. Other people just want to be nice, and won't shoot you at all, and even invite you in for lemonade.

People are like that everywhere. That is something you learn from walking across the country. It's a general statement but it's something one doesn't quite believe until one actually sees it for one's self.

The fruit that I ate for breakfast and lunch was stolen, insofar as something that grows on a tree which grows from the planet can be stolen. But those trees were on *private property*, and so was the fruit.

I know because I saw the sign on the fence.

And then I looked around and, seeing I was alone, climbed over the fence, picked the fruit, and ate it as I walked down the road. I don't remember what fruit I had that particular day, because I ate a lot of fruit during the next few days. Peaches and oranges, probably. I eat a lot of peaches and oranges. Oranges are strong in vitamin C and are very refreshing since they are so full of juice. And one can toss the peel on the ground without guilt, because ants will take care of it. I don't know what peaches's virtues are. All I know about peaches is that they are good. And the way I got them, they were also free.

Another thing that I learned from my brief time in remote areas of the country is that people in rural areas don't care about the things people in big cities worry about. People in big cities have unique concerns, and people in rural areas have no direct equivalent. People in rural areas don't worry about trade and stock markets; they worry about their crops and livestock. They don't watch movie stars or business people or politicians on television; they watch weather reports and game shows. They don't worry about getting shot out on the streets; they worry about getting run over by a plow on accident.

If you ever travel through these rural portions of the country, you should not hesitate to stop in at local shoppes. Usually the people who run them are all related, because they are family businesses. Usually they are friendly because they don't see many strangers, since everyone who lives in the area knows everyone else, because there are so few people around. I know all of this because every proprietor of every store I entered told me so.

Chapter Seventeen

There was a general store that sold snake skin garments. no one in the store found anything wrong with that. In fact, the owner himself was wearing a snakeskin belt. His wife was at the cash register, and she was co-owner. There was a big glass jar full of cucumbers, which were in various stages of pickling. There were dried fruits and fresh fruits.

I had gone in to ask to use their restroom and to buy some water to drink on my journey. It was very hot, as usual, and I'd been walking all day. They let me use their restroom, and there were lots of wooden ducks in the restroom as decoration, and they asked me where I was from and what was I doing so far out west? I told them I was from the prospering city of Philadelphia, which is not true, and I said I was visiting relatives out west, which is also not true. They sold me a pickle, which was home-made. It was good and not completely pickled yet. It tasted very authentic. They sold me a large bottle of water. And then I left. They had also wanted to sell me a shot glass that had an inscription on it that said

God is a Rocky Mountains Hillbilly

which is not true, and they said it would make a nice souvenir to show my relatives out west, but I said I didn't believe God was in fact from the Rocky Mountains, and I didn't buy it.

I remember this store well because the people were so friendly, and I'd never seen a restroom decorated with wooden ducks before. Most of the store was wooden, in fact. The floor creaked when I walked on it, and it sounded hollow. If you are ever in this area and see a little wooden shopped called "General Store: Drygoods and Produce" then I urge you to stop in for some of the local flavour, and try a pickle, and ask to use their restroom.

My last recommendation as a travel guide is a little blue building I found that evening in a small town. It was next to a motel, which I think was called "Motor Inn", and it is a diner with four seats at the counter and only six or seven tables in the dining area. There are blue plaid curtains on the windows. It's a wooden building that has been painted sky blue. You cannot miss it.

I took a seat at the counter and saw that the restaurant was empty. There wasn't anyone behind the counter, either. I thought the little shoppe had closed down, until a large friendly dark woman, with beautiful hair that writhed gently as she walked, came from the back room and asked what I wanted to eat. She showed me a menu. It was hand-written, but very neatly done. I ordered pancakes, although the menu called them "flapjacks" or "slapjacks"; I could not tell because it was handwritten in very fancy lettering. She made my pancakes right there in front of me, while I watched. She cooked them on the griddle and even heated syrup for me. She said it was real maple syrup. Real maple syrup is very sweet and should not be used in excess. She told me so, and she was right.

She asked me why I hadn't heard of real maple syrup before, and didn't they have that on the East Coast? I said no and how did she know I was from the East Coast? She said she could tell by the way I talked, and I said I knew I didn't talk like people in that town but that I didn't know people could tell where I was from just by hearing me speak.

As I ate my pancakes, she talked to me and washed dishes. The pancakes were as large as the plate, and they were very good. I had a lot of butter on them.

I asked her if she had made the butter herself, and she said no, she had bought it at the local supermarket. She had gotten it at a very good price, and she told me that if I clipped coupons out of the newspaper, I could save almost five dollars a week.

For sake of accurate research, I inquired about the diner's history. It is a lucky thing I did. Remember that this diner is a blue building, next to a motel, and is well worth the visit. This establishment was clean and well decorated and the food was good. The pancakes did not cost a dollar. They cost two dollars and seventy-five cents, but it was worth it. I drank orange juice, too, and that was cheap, although I forgot to make a note of the exact price.

She said the diner had been in her family for five generations, which makes it very old indeed. She actually lived in the back. The diner was in fact *private property*, unlike most restaurants, which are actually public places. She said most of the little amount of business she got was from people staying at the motel, and from people who worked in the area.

She asked me what the East Coast was like and said she had never been there. She asked a lot about New York City, because many people think it's the most important city in the nation. People who live there think so, too. I told her the usual story about New York City; it was busy, and big, and people there were rude but not too bad, and things like that, which everyone just expects to hear about the city. If you tell them anything else, they will make you say these other things through conversation.

For instance, if you say that New York City isn't really such a big place, compared to São Paulo and places like that, then they will say that this may be true, but they'll bet that New York City's pretty big compared to where ever they live. And then you would have to agree, and so they are happy, because you have said that New York City was a large city.

If you insist that people in New York City are very friendly, they will insist that they had heard otherwise until you finally give in and agree that people in New York City are very mean. Evil, even.

The lady who ran the restaurant said she was saving up her money so that she could start a Bed And Breakfast somewhere out East. She said she would sell her restaurant to the motel next door and move to New England, which was a term I hadn't heard in years. I told her so, and she said that was what everyone called the Northeast. I told her no one on the East Coast called it that, not even the people who live there, and I should know because I lived out EAST.

East. It's just a word.

I told her also that the nation's government had dissolved, that it no longer existed, and that whatever remained was a façade. She was dismal when she heard the news, and then a little indignant. She said she had watched The News that morning, and again that afternoon and that the President Himself had given a press conference about education and employment. She said the President Himself had said education from now on would be geared only toward specific vocations, so once a student is out of school they would go right into their careers.

It would keep the kids out of trouble.

That's what the President Himself said.

So she believed it.

Chapter Eighteen

The President Himself also said schools would no longer be co-ed, which is an abbreviated term meaning the integration of genders. It is short for co-educational. Neither the abbreviated term or the full word has anything to do with genders, but people still use it for that purpose. Words will mean what people want them to mean. For instance, one time I asked a friend to buy me a fucking milkshake. I meant, of course, a normal milkshake, but my friend's mother was very much offended and asked me why I had cursed. Of course I had not cursed anyone or anything. I would not even know how to place a curse on someone if I wanted to, which I do not. The word FUCK to most people does not have an exact meaning; it is a term used for emphasis in most cases, unless it is used in a specific context.

For instance, if someone says that they are going to go to bed and fuck, then they are not using the word for emphasis. If they say they are going to fucking bed, then they are using it for emphasis.

Context is not beside the point. I have heard the word FUCK uttered many times and I have never been offended by it. Nor by terms like BLOODCLOT and DAMN and BITCH. A friend of mine once called me a bitch. I knew she was not actually expressing animosity toward me, and so I called her a bitch, and we were both very happy, and we probably went out to buy a fucking milkshake or two. On the other hand, I have heard very common words like PAL and THANKS A LOT uttered with such spite that they were far worse than BITCH or anything like it.

A very rich man wanted a cup of coffee once, and he went to a café and asked for coffee, but they were still making the coffee, and there would be a five minute wait. The very rich man was in a very big hurry and could not wait five minutes for coffee, so he said to the restaurant owner "Thanks, pal." He was not sincere in calling the owner his PAL. In fact, his voice was so cruel, that I think if someone had come by and called the owner a BLOODY SOD it probably would have cheered him up. I myself was very tempted to call him a MOTHERFUCKER just to lift his spirits.

Co-ed schools were no more, the lady said. I still do not know if she was correct. She said from now on, all schools both public and private would have to be segregated by gender. There would be schools for boys and schools for girls, and never shall the twain meet.

The President also said that girls would have to start covering their hair in school, and he and the First Lady (a term used for a President's wife, to make them feel good about themselves, since women still can't really expect to be President) hoped they would continue to cover their hair as a regular habit outside of school.

The First Lady stepped onto stage and she was wearing a cloth over her hair. She modeled it. Everyone clapped. It had been made for her by a famous Italian fashion designer. It had cost her a fortune.

This is what the lady in the restaurant told me. I do not know if it is true. If it is true, then it looks like humans are on the road to recovery at last, and soon everyone will be happily segregated, and they will buy designer head-dresses. If it is not true, then I guess anarchy really does reign, and all that will be different is that people won't buy expensive designer head-dresses.

I asked the lady why she wanted to open up a Bed And Breakfast on the East Coast and she said because she'd always wanted to. She said Bed And Breakfasts were very popular in the East. She said she liked being a hostess to people. She said she guesses she was just raised that way.

I don't like to be hostess. If I had invited someone to my house, if I had a house, and if I had someone to invite over to it, they would have to do everything themselves. I would offer them a drink, and then make them go get it themselves, and since they are on the way, they should make me one too.

Some people just like to be hosts, I guess. It must be the way they were raised. They must feel their home is sacred, and that they are offering their body and blood. I do not believe this. If I had a house, I would maintain it as necessary, but a guest is just a guest and there isn't any reason that I see to serve the guest as a humble servant. If they don't want to be there, then they shouldn't be there, and acting like their servant isn't going to change their mind. If they want to be there, then they won't need you to act like a humble servant, because they would be there whether you served them or not.

The lady, my hostess, says many people go to the East for vacations, and they needed a comfortable place to stay, but what they really wanted was a *home away from home*. These sound like magic words. As a hostess of a Bed And Breakfast, it would be her job to sweep up their scraps of food and crumbs, to clean their bathrooms, and to launder their sheets and clothes, and to cook their meals. Some people just love to stay busy, I suspect. They think it is *fun* to be busy.

A very very very very long time ago in a far away land called Hellas (Greece) there was a cosmic phone booth called The Oracle, which was in a place called Delphi. And people would go there to ask questions and receive puzzling answers in return. They did not ask God directly; they asked a priestess, who then spoke for God. This is a job I would like to have. It would be better than being a hostess.

I would have accepted this job if I'd lived then. The priestesses were very young ladies, and they usually died young, too. No one now knows why. Some people who are called Experts, which is another term which has no real meaning, say that the young ladies spent too much time in caves at Delphi and it was bad for their health. Other people said the young ladies took drugs in order to speak effectively for God, and it killed them after a while. Some say the responsibility of speaking for God was too great a burden for a mortal to bear for long. Some say the responsibility was of such a spiritual nature that their time on Earth just wasn't important by comparison.

Knowing this, I still would have accepted the job. I would be kept busy, but I would be doing something I enjoy. I would rather speak for God and die young than run a Bed And Breakfast.

I asked the lady behind the counter if she would rather be a vestal virgin or a hostess at a Bed And Breakfast. She said she was past being a vestal virgin. I don't think she understood my question.

She asked if I was rich and did I want to buy her restaurant? I said no. She laughed, and so did I, because she was a cheerful and optimistic person, and sometimes that can be a very funny thing.

A man came into the restaurant and said hello politely and said hello to the lady behind the counter. He was familiar with her, and I could tell by their conversation. He didn't say anything more to me, because he didn't know me.

He was a police officer, or a judge, or both. This much I gathered from his conversation with the hostess. So I asked him if it was true that the town's local government had dissolved. He said I was wrong to think so, and wanted to know where I'd heard it. I told him I'd heard talk about it, which was not true but satisfied him. He said there wasn't much to do in the town as far as law enforcement went, but there were still laws to make. And sometimes they got drunk drivers and barroom brawls.

He said to the hostess isn't that right. She said yes, it was. I believe them.

Chapter Nineteen

A group of young women passed by the restaurant windows and we watched them pass. Mr. John E. Law (not his real name, as far as I know) commented that the people of the town were *Basically Good Folk*, and that they all Minded Their Own Business.

The young women had been wearing the latest fashions, and lots of make-up, and they all looked very nice and very hot. According to historians, the term HOT once was a slang term for "sexually attractive" but I can't imagine anyone using the word in this manner. Heat is too real and too persistent to allow for alternate, complimentary meanings.

I find that most women -- myself included sometimes -- dress very theatrically. They create outfits based on popular ideas. They will wear a dress that suggests the turn of the century, or a skirt and shoes called penny loafers to suggest the time on this Earth when Mr. Elvis Presley reigned, or they will wear tight clothes that glow to suggest modernity. I was sitting in the restaurant in shorts and a t-shirt, so at the time I was not guilty of this hyperbolic creativity, but I had been,and probably I have been since.

To pass time, I sometimes imagine a world in which men dress as extravagantly as women, with fashions stemming from common male fantasies. I picture what fashions might evolve from the male mind, if that male were inclined to create costumes suggestive of how he sees himself, or how he wants to be seen by others. Something that would suggest what he wants his nature to be. Presently it seems that men's fashions are based on either the classic Suit And Tie motif or they are outfits which complement current women's fashion. If men dressed in accordance to their own mental images of themselves, as women often do, I suspect one would find men wearing gladiator costumes and spaceman uniforms and top-secret super-agent uniforms, and maybe even comic book super hero suits. You never know what might turn up.

It is not much more absurd than a woman's ball gown or short skirt. You should not think so.

The girls who passed by the window made me think long and hard. Ancient gods they were

to whom men and women sacrificed whatever selfless depression that found them wandering through what could pass as a desert or a land of total sunless pitch. The moment is as invisible as the future, and only the embarrassing past remains as a memory of a question:

Why?

Of course no answer is given.

I was still sitting alone, I was drinking only my juice, because alcohol hadn't held an appeal for me for years. I remembered scenes of my past but nothing in continuity. What must have surely been a day-long family excursion was invariably reduced in my mind to a five second moving photograph. What must have involved ten people or more became a one- or two-person dialogue.

I hadn't asked to be a slave to memories. I hadn't asked to be free of them. I hadn't asked for memories at all. Foresight is no more than hindsight recycled and applied to possible futures. The past is all that is known, so it is all one has on which to base one's expectations for the future. This is something I realised while drinking my juice. I assumed for the time being that I had a mother and father, so I then assumed that I must have been taught certain ideas and mannerisms. But for all my snapshot memories, I found it impossible to apply anything so long ago to what might come.

I was in the dark.

A long time ago, in ancient times, oracles talked to people in riddles. And they never gave easy answers. Usually the answers were not understood until after a terrible mistake has been made, and the stunned and confused person looked back and scratched his head and said *So That's Where I Went Wrong!*

People are always looking back. And they are often seen standing on the side of a city street, getting in peoples's way, and scratching their heads, saying *So That's Where I Went Wrong!*

I have tried to apply my snapshot memories to the future, and I have also scratched my head, telling myself those magical words, and they made me feel like I'd learned something. Just saying *So That's Where I Went Wrong!* made you think you'd really learned a lesson. And then you try to apply that lesson to the future, and you end up scratching your head saying it all over again, and feeling very good about it. People are always looking back to go forward.

The illustration there is clear.

The illustrations on the napkins in the restaurant were poorly done.

They were meant to look like quilted designs, to make people think they remembered Country Life, which was something that was mythically peaceful and perfect, and something that no one had actually experienced. It was a modern myth, so a rich company had printed references to the myth on their products.

Huckleberry Finn.

Rather, Tom Sawyer. Huckleberry Finn is a much better book than Tom Sawyer, and it is more serious. I have read Huckleberry Finn three times.

I do not mind being alone in crowded places because then being alone is a comfort. It is a real comfort. So I was comforted when the lady at the restaurant and the police officer started to forget about me.

I sometimes hear music when I am alone.

Traveling makes you feel like you are not just alone, but that you are making progress alone. There is an allegorical meaning to Homer's The Odyssey that was lost upon most people. There is evidence, however, that this epic was actually seen mostly as an allegory even in ancient Greece, because Plato in The Republic wrote that the old epics, Homer included, were in fact not to be taken literally. So when the gods are fighting one another in those epics, even the Greeks didn't believe it actually was taking place in a literal sense. So even Plato, a citizen of ancient Greece, did not view Homer's stories as realistic.

Neither, by the way, did an ancient historian named Thucydides, but that is another matter.

Chapter Twenty

I could have been on an odyssey myself. Like Huckleberry Finn. Or a dozen of popular literature's main characters who have to avenge their fathers or save their lover or solve a mystery. They have to find something to make everything better. There are many goals in works of fiction, which is why it is called Fiction.

For years now people have been abandoning their posts. It doesn't matter where they work, they just abandon their posts, and they think they might have a mission more important, or else they once thought they were on a mission but then one day lost faith in that belief.

And sometimes the opposite happens. People won't stop even when it is clear they are no longer needed. The newspaper featured a *human interest* story about a bus driver in downtown Charleston, which was once a fairly busy little city in the lower Northern half of the country. no one ever rode the bus any more, because the city was pretty much dead. But that bus driver drove his bus route every day any way.

The newspaper presented the story with a strong sense of pride and dignity. They said the bus driver was a true patriot. They said he was a noble representative of his city, which was pretty much dead any way.

The bus driver told the reporters that he hadn't had a passenger in three years, without exception. Not one passenger on his bus in three years. Neither had he missed a day's work. So if he worked five days a week for fifty-two weeks a year for three years, that means in seven-hundred and eighty days of driving his bus, he had zero passengers. Nor had he received a pay cheque in all of that time, since the bus authority in the city had closed down a few years earlier.

It would have been four years without a passenger, except that on Christmas Eve four years ago the bus had been flagged down by a hopelessly lost traveler standing shivering in the snow. The bus driver gave him a free ride across town. The bus driver said that normally this as not allowed but seeing as it was Christmas Eve, he made an exception. He said buses aren't taxis, and they aren't for hitch-hikers, either.

Many people have lost interest in careers. They feel estranged from society. That is what the psychologists say, so I guess it must be true. Sociologists, incidentally, say that society feels estranged from society. So I guess that's true, too.

One minute, there would be a toll collector at a booth on a highway, and then the next minute there would be a toll collector walking down that highway, curious for the first time in her life to see what exactly she had been collecting all of that money for. It must be something good for so many cars to pay to see every day. Day in, and day out.

And also there was a college professor who realised he was finally tired of repeating the same quasi-religious babble about history and science and math year after year, so one day he didn't show for class, and every day thereafter. The students, I suspect, waited until after the semester was over to report him missing.

They found him. But not for a year. One of his former students had been hiking, and came across him by pure chance. He was living in a log cabin in a state park. He had changed his name to The Brook That Babbles, and he preached to the forest nymphs, in whom he sincerely believed, against history and science and math, in which he sincerely did not believe.

Suburban workers often decide to just stay home and barbecue all day long. They cook dead cows on grills all day, and refuse to acknowledge that The Office existed. They said every day that it was July Fourth, and they believed it, too.

Holidays are difficult to keep, since most people have rather forgotten what they are for or that they existed. Old holidays are mostly pretty much gone. Christmas remains, and children still believe in Santa Claus. Or Papa Noël or whatever they call him in their country. July Fourth is gone but many people still believe in it. Other holidays are so abandoned that people don't even remember their names. All they know is that once on a certain day there was a holiday for some reason. In November some people still have a feast called Thanksgiving, but this is mostly just in rural areas. They dress in suits and ties, and they eat dead birds, and they pretend to be very happy and thankful. And maybe they really are.

Most people don't really need holidays now, because when someone wants to take a day off from work, they do. It isn't as if there is a long line of people waiting around to take their place at the job.

I know through certain reliable sources that once Work was sort of a national religion. People worked even if they were what was then called a Rich Bastard. And they would just keep on making more and more money, and they never knew what to do with it all. If they did not spend it, the government would take it. I can't remember the last time the government collected taxes. They sure did then, though. So the rich people would buy houses and cars and prostitutes and still couldn't get rid of all that money, but still they went to work each day. Day in, and day out.

I have almost no money. What I do have, I carry with me in my back pocket, like a wallet. I have never worked a day in my life. When I was young, my family must have paid for everything; that is usually the way things go when you're a kid. And then when I got older, I had a bank account that had been created in my name when I was born. And there was money there, and there had been money there for my entire life, and it had been collecting interest from the bank. Now what is left of that money resides snugly in my back pocket, like a wallet. There may be more money sitting around with my name on it, but I don't know. My family may have been rich, but I don't know for sure. I know my grandfather sure is famous, and usually if you're famous, you're rich. But I really just don't know for sure.

I don't ever want to work. That is one thing I know for sure.

People once called this attitude Lazy, or Being A Bum. But now it is pretty common.

Sometimes when there is no clear point to life, someone will try to find clarity by placing importance upon smaller elements within their life. They will find eighteen good reasons to think life is really worth living.

They might find twenty-eight cents in their pocket and say "There must be a reason I have twenty-eight cents, and not twenty-seven or twenty-nine." And they will ponder this until they've built an entire philosophy around it, and they will say that now their life makes sense and has meaning and everything is clear.

There can be profundity in simplicity.

I once tried to write haiku, which is a popular form of japanese poetry that stemmed from the earlier form of hokku, and it is not as easy as it looks. This is just one more reason I like haiku: because it is deceptively complex. It seems simple, but it is not.

There was a haiku written across the street. A blind man had acquired two albino cobras, and he kept them in a large aquarium in his living room. For five dollars, he would let you inside and show you the two albino cobras. It was the town's small claim to fame and had even been mentioned in a local promotional tourist guide.

I don't know if he knew that his sign was written in haiku. It was painted blue, with yellow letters. It said:

Albino Cobras See them alive and deadly Five dollars per guest

I had no interest in seeing two albino cobras. It was a good thing, too, because I didn't really have five dollars to throw away on something like that. I had just spent a fair amount of money on my meal.

But there were more than a few people who paid to see those albino cobras. The lady behind the counter said she had. So did the lawman. He said he didn't believe they were really albinos. He said the man had them under a black light, and it only made them look albino. The lady behind the counter said she had heard he found the cobras in South America, in the Amazon, and smuggled them back into this fine land. She said they were worth millions of dollars, but he thought he was really lucky to charge people five dollars each. She said he was the village idiot.

I wondered who had blinded him, and why. But I didn't ask. The question would have been indiscreet, especially in front of the lawman.

Those cobras belonged to that blind man. They were his *private property* and if you wanted to see them, you had to pay five dollars. If anyone tried to see the *private property* without paying him, he would probably shoot at them. I've seen blind men shoot with remarkable accuracy. Actually, I have not actually seen it for myself, but I've heard about it.

The restaurant I was sitting in was also *private property*. The lady behind the counter could refuse to admit anyone she wanted to. It was not a public establishment. Probably there are laws against that but no one really cares. The restaurant hadn't been inspected for sanitation in years. On the East Coast, you wouldn't see a restaurant without their business license and inspection certificates posted on the wall like an award.

> I paid my bill and hit the road even though it
> was getting late.

I didn't really want to spend $$money$$ on a hotel room. So I thought I'd find some *private property* and sleep on its outskirts.

I have been shot with salt. I was on *private property* and the owner saw me from across the field. Without any warning at all, he shot and hit me in the back. He had loaded his shotgun with salt. It stings and leaves a mark but it does not do serious damage. It's a good way for people to shoot things and cause a good deal of pain and alarm without actually doing serious damage. This kind of activity is usually called Good Clean *Fun*, because it does not really destroy anything. Normal *fun* is more destructive.

Lucky for me, I didn't have anyone to care for, or anyone who cared for me, so I had no time schedule. I could come and go as I pleased. I could travel from the restaurant and sleep in an open field with bugs and field mice and stray dogs and cats and wake up at dawn and go right on traveling. If you have someone to make life seem like it's got a meaning, then you tend to do less things like this, and you sit home and just enjoy being around that person. That's the ideal, any way.

Often the ideal and the reality of a situation are very different.

The reality of my situation was that I was walking right past the house of live-and-deadly albino cobras, right past the haiku sign, and right past the blind man selling tickets into his living room. He heard or sensed that I was near, and he said Would I like to buy a ticket to see the only two albino cobras in the world, Miss? I said no. I don't know how he knew I was a 'Miss' and not a 'Mister'.

A very long time ago, in ancient civilisations, blind people were sometimes thought to possess supernatural powers. Maybe they did then, but they sure don't now. There are just too many of them to be considered gifted.

I asked him how he had lost his vision. And if you had been there, you would not have believed how his eager smile faded away. And he said exactly this: "Why don't you just leave me alone?"

I sure did feel bad.

He probably deserved it. It isn't my fault that a girl felt the need to blind him. Probably he has no one to blame but himself.

I left him alone. I kept on walking. I didn't want to hurt his feelings any more.

I was fortunate enough to come across a rest area. Not many people use rest areas any more, but when I was younger, and before that, rest areas were havens for weary middle-class travelers. They would drive on the freeways and when they needed to rest from driving, they would stop at a rest area, and sit down and eat processed lunch meat from cans, which they always had in little coolers, to save on money for food on the road, and drink juice from cans or boxes, and they would relax and feel really good about the way things were going. They would sigh and pat their bellies and say things like "What a good day it's been."

or "We've made good time to-day!"

or "It's been such a day, what could possibly go wrong?"

or "It sure is nice to *get away from it all*!"

Magic words.

Then they would get back into their cars and drive away, leaving lots of empty cans and boxes and plastic forks to commemorate their passage, their presence. Rest areas were like an oasis.

Chapter Twenty-One

And now it was my own personal oasis. I had it all to myself. When I got there, I used the restroom, and washed up. There was soap in the dispensers. Someone sure was dedicated to that rest area. I really washed up well. Since no one else was around, I undressed and gave myself quite a scrubbing until I was squeaky clean. In fact, it could be said with no small degree of accuracy that I washed until I felt like new, because that is how I felt afterwards:

Like New.

I felt like a new woman until something happened that made me feel that I hadn't just washed: after I dressed, and when I turned to leave the bathroom, and I saw a man standing in the doorway. It was the janitor of the rest area, in fact. I had caught him as he was moving to leave.

He had been watching me the whole entire time. I could tell just by looking at him.

Probably the only sense of meaning in his life any more was filling up soap dispensers and replenishing rolls of paper towels, and generally maintaining the upkeep of that abandoned rest area. He did these things every day, even though no one ever came to his rest area any more.

I could tell he had been watching me because of the look on his face. He was considering running, but to do that would be to admit his guilt, so he stayed in the doorway.

He was watching me still. Like a cat watches a mouse.

He thought that I was going to attack him with sexual passion. This is what he thought, and let there be no mistake about it. He thought that since he'd watched me bathe, then we were friends. That I would make him fuck me.

I don't suppose that he had ever been more mistaken than he was at that point in his life. The basis for this assumption will become clear shortly.

When I looked at him, I confess that I was mortified at first, and not just a little upset at having been spied upon.

He didn't say anything, of course. He just tugged at his suspenders and kicked at a loose terra cotta tile in the floor. And he watched me still. He really did believe that he had become a friend to me. I really had nothing to say to him at all, by way of either forgiveness or of indignation. So I didn't say anything.

Standing there, guilty of having secretly watched me bathe, all he could manage to say was "I put the soap in the machines."

That was the last thing he said on God's good green Earth.

His brain was toasted within a matter of seconds. He didn't even have time to notice, I suspect, that he'd been blinded seconds prior to that, because after I burnt out his retinas, I just let my eyes dwell, and after that the janitor fell to the floor, face first.

It is nothing I haven't seen before.

They say women rarely faint at the sight of blood because blood is such a part of a woman's life. So a man's nose exploding on the bathroom tiles had little or no effect upon me.

And a man without retinas or a functioning brain falling to the ground is not so unusual in life, either.

Most people are afraid to take their clothes off if they think someone is watching. But sometimes you just can't worry about things like that. Being seen without clothes on is not like dying; you are still alive when it's all over. And if you want, you can always just burn out the eyes of the person who saw you, and then they will actually try to not remember how you looked without clothes on, because the memory will become an unpleasant one, since it is also how they lost their vision. This tactic should work well, although I admit I have not had the occasion to try it. Sometimes it is best just to lay the man to his eternal rest.

So then I sat down at a picnic bench.

It was on a pavilion, in the shade, and I opened up a can of peaches, which I'd bought for a few cents, a mile back at a small gas convenience store along the road. I ate, and then I slept. These are two essential things that everyone must do in life. There are more things that are essential, but these two are what I did at that time.

I awoke later, and probably ate more. One does these things.

Chapter Twenty-Two

When I was a little girl, I saw a leaf covered with beads of rain, and as a bead hung tenuously from the tip of the leaf, I saw the whole world compressed inside of it. And I thought this must be the handwriting of angels, because even though I didn't know what an angel's alphabet looks like, I assumed those beautiful, complete crystal balls must be it.

When I cannot believe in something, I become physically ill. When I know something that I do not want to believe, I pretend it was just a dream. That helps deal with these moments in life which, if taken as they actually occurred , could upset the entire way one lives.

To preserve disbelief, one may choose to think of an upsetting event as a mere dream or illusion

like a hummingbird in the corner of the eye

seems only for a moment as it hovers, like a little angel floating through the flowers.

It takes pages and pages of symbols and letters and words to express just one simple idea. But not for everyone. There are letters upon leaves in the morning that reflect the entire sky, and words that encapsulate an entire forest. These are thoughts that come to my head as I travel.

Angels travel. And they leave a mark upon the ground they cross.

Chasing butterflies as a child, I came to understand that when something is unobtainable, it is frustrating. But probably once you obtain it, you wouldn't know what to do with it. So to try to find an angel traveling across the country would be useless, and so would it be to try to decipher their writing.

I tell the truth when I confess that as I walked, no longer could I believe in sanity or order, since such a precedence had been set for the definitions that were ideals without forms that resembled the ideals. I attacked a figurehead, like the concept of freedom under a ruling class. Now gone.

Sitting in an empty room, sometimes my thoughts would echo off of the blank walls,

and wandered across the floor

   intermingling with my shadow

and the shadows of the leaves.

Light from the window reveals an angel, once in a dream, who spoke, but in a foreign tongue that I could not understand.

A man visiting this fine land once asked me for directions. He said "You will tell I how to go to 59th Street?" I spent an hour explaining to him how to reach his destination. I drew a map on a napkin. I provided elaborate descriptions of notable landmarks along the way.

After I had finished, he said "You will tell I how to go to 59th Street?"

He had not understood a word I had said.

Communication is a problem to this day. Languages have been broken down into pictures like

and still no one understands what anyone is saying.

Chapter
Twenty-Two

Much less what an angel is saying.

Whether in silence or chaotic noise, the mind concentrates largely upon itself, and it gets lost there, and I become physically ill in my confusion. This is a very real form of communication. It's the one message that cannot be misunderstood.

And so when angels speak, sometimes people just get sick.

Sometimes things take you by surprise. A rainy day that cools everything off, when before there hadn't been a cloud in the sky. A person who befriends you when before you had barely even noticed them. Ideas occur without warning or explanation. It is called "out of thin air" or "pulling a rabbit out of a hat".

It's magic.

Magic exists in many forms. I saw a magic show when I was a little girl, and I believed it. Now I am older and I believe in magic of different sorts. Such as when someone smiles and says something nice to me for no reason at all.

Silly things.

Like "You're a great person to be around."

and "I like those shoes you're wearing."

and "You seem to be an intelligent person..."

and "I'd like you're opinion on something..."

It's magic.

Even apocalyptic.

I met a magic person once, and I know he had magic because he said magic words, and even though there were no clouds in the sky in the morning, it rained that night, and though we didn't know each other before that day that we met, we were friends by sundown.

He was sitting at a table in a roadhouse. The outside was lit in blue neon. The inside was lit in blue, too. There was music, and the smell of smoke and beer and other forms of harder liquor. The first words he spoke to me were these: "I no longer believe in the power of Reason."

These are powerful words of introduction, when often "Hi" and "Good Evening" were pretty much as good as it gets.

Much better than the old mythological "Can I buy you a drink?" -- which, although I have never heard this actually used -- I certainly have heard that it once was the most popular greeting in bars long ago.

Greetings are very difficult to do. Sometimes they are the hardest things to do. That is why I am not too dedicated to greetings. I say simple things as greetings and expect no response. Sometimes a person responds. Sometimes they do not.

When I found the roadhouse it was by a glow in the horizon. At first I thought that the aliens were finally landing. Why shouldn't they? I was out on an empty road in a barren desert, and it was dusk, so I thought the aliens might think that was a good time to land. I assume they would want to land at night to provide themselves plenty of time to cover their spaceship and maybe put on disguises or just walk around unseen.

But it was not the aliens. This I discovered as soon as I had walked another half mile and saw the source of the blue glow. It was, of course, just the lone roadhouse; a lone building along the road. There wasn't another building in sight, in fact. The blue lights formed letters. They said: LIQUOR LIQUOR LIQUOR. That is all they said.

There were no women in the bar. There were only men, and it looked like they were all hard workers, and hated their jobs, and mostly they were all drunk. But at least they were working. That is something to admire. One cannot fault a hard worker for working hard.

When I walked in through those glass doors, no one even noticed me. I didn't order a drink. I didn't sit at the bar. I walked across the room in time with the beat of the music and took a seat at an empty table. Except it wasn't empty. I didn't notice it, but I had taken a seat at someone's table. The other person at the table was soon to become a good friend.

And he saw my eyes glowing in the darkness, and he was not afraid.

That was when he said these words: "I no longer believe in the power of Reason."

Then he said: "God knows what god is doing."

He was staring into his drink, which was sitting upon the table before him, like a black hole. I have now begun to suspect that he did not believe it was real. I know for a fact that he did not believe that I was real. Because he had lost confidence in his senses. He believed, and still does, I imagine, that I existed only as reflections exist upon the surface of a lake, or the lights reflected in his drink.

I have heard that little babies, when set upon a glass table that is partially covered with a blanket, will not venture off of the blanket, because it is too young and too stupid to understand that the glass actually exists and it will not fall to the ground.

Stumbling through life, it occurs to many people that they may be walking on glass.

So when he spoke to me, he had no fear of sounding silly or moody.

In fact,

when I am feeling ill

I rarely believe anything is real.

I feel ill when I have read or heard of something that I find impossible to believe, so naturally I don't believe anything is real while I'm ill.

When people have hang-overs from too much alcohol, they rarely believe anything outside of their own headache is real. They stumble down the street smacking their lips and massaging their temples, and when a car screeches to a halt and curses and complains and shakes its fists, they don't even notice that they almost had been flattened across the road. They don't believe in the external world at all; so the road and the car mean nothing to them.

The man at the table was suffering from too much alcohol. His head felt like it was floating around the roadhouse, like the lights floating in his drinks. He's not a man who is aware of much. He knows simple things, like: to live, one must eat. And: alcohol makes everything unreal. And: there is peace in sleep. And: life is not as impressive as all the ads make it out to be.

Business is business. It always has been and, I suspect, always will be. It is the driving force behind most everything within a society. People like money, and through business comes money. The worst thing that could ever happen to business is that people would stop believing life can be *fun*, because then people will not believe in the ads, and they will stop buying useless things and giving business all of their money. This is why ads make life look so good. They make it look like something you would really want to buy.

For business to really work, there also should be a strong sense of ownership. You have to own what you buy, and rich businesspeople need to own things, too. Everyone has to own things. So governments write long legal papers and constitutions to prove that all of these things that have been bought are really owned. If it were not so, then people wouldn't feel they were really getting their money's worth.

Not many people know this, but most western countries were established because businesspeople and governments thought it would be a good way to make money on sugar. So they killed native people and set up sugar farms. That is why western nations to-day exist.

Ads are sometimes good to make people think that life was a really good thing, and like they could get their money's worth. Beer ads are best at this. This is probably why the roadhouse was selling so much beer that night. A new ad had just come out, and it was telling people that beer made life worth living. So people bought lots of beer, and some men within that very roadhouse did believe that life was really worth living.

My friend at the table sure didn't think so. He's bought about as much beer as anyone I know, and so far life still wasn't *fun*.

In fact, businesspeople would be very disappointed in my friend across the table. He didn't really buy much of anything any more. He bought food, and beer, but that is just about all. He owned five pairs of pants and seven shirts and as many socks and shorts, and a pair of shoes. That was all he needed. He rented a little trailer home not far from the roadhouse. And he owned a lot of very interesting books, which in fact would have gotten him into a lot of trouble if anyone had actually cared enough to notice what kind of literature he had immersed himself in.

He read a lot of Emma Goldman, and he did not believe in governments. He also did not believe in business. Or violence. In fact, he didn't really believe in much at all. As I have said, he did not even believe in me, and I became his *best friend*.

I had no competition.

Chapter Twenty-Three

To feel one's head swimming through the smoke filled air of a roadhouse can be very disorienting. It was a long time before my friend across the table spoke again. He put a hand to his head and he took time to gather his wits.

People kill just to gather their wits. And he did it just as an afterthought to drunkenness. He'd smuggled a little bit of sanity with him when he had come in through that door.

He'd been there all evening, sitting in that same spot, just drinking beer slowly. He had to work to-morrow, and he was not looking forward to working to-morrow, because the men he worked with did not like him, in part because he did not believe that they were real. If he only would believe that they actually existed, they might have like him a little more.

He could verify through his senses that he existed, and he'd read Descartes, but he had no proof that anything around him was real. He felt like he'd been set upon a spinning wheel which spun around completely every twenty-four hours, and he couldn't get off, and he just had to sit on the wheel and watch the same pictures pass by as he spun around. The first picture he saw was his own sleepy face, shaving. Then there was a picture of the shower, then coffee by the roadside, waiting for his carpool of fellow employees. Then there were pictures of work, and then the bar, and then bed, and then it all happened again.

The pictures were like clockwork. They never failed. They never altered.

For the past year, he felt that he'd been living the same day over and over. Once his boss had brought him into an office and yelled at him for two hours straight. This had been a new picture, but not so significant to suggest that it was something revolutionary or important. It was a variation on a theme.

I was a variation on a theme. With my glowing eyes, sitting across the table from him, I was just a reflection in his glass.

On his arm he had a tattoo: it was an "A" in a circle. That is the symbol for Anarchism. no one ever bothered him about his tattoo, because no one cared enough to be offended or indignant. That is called Apathy, and it is a friend to many.

You may be wondering how I know all of this about him, and you may even think I might just be making it all up to make an interesting story. Well, I can tell you how I know so much about him: he told me, later that same night.

He drew symbols in the puddle of water around his glass. This is what he was doing on the outside but it was completely separate from what was happening on the inside. I know this because I could read his thoughts. I stared at him, and he was unaware of my stare, and when this happens, I can usually read a person's mind. I read his mind until he became aware that I was watching him.

So while he was drawing things in water on the table with his finger, lazily, I was actively reading his each and every thought. This is not a power that everyone has; it is something that I discovered when I was a young girl.

Here is what he was really thinking:

"How did I become so alone?"

"Have I ever been un-alone?"

"Why do I fear being alone?"

"What can I do to become un-alone?"

And then he repeated the same thing, word for word, over and over again, each time emphasising a different word within each sentence. He was studying the ideas. He was really meditating on those questions.

He stopped when he saw that I was watching him. He took a drink. I don't know if he knows I had read his mind. I have not asked, because to ask the question would be to confess of the act. For instance, if I were to ask "Do you know I once read your mind?" then obviously either an affirmative or a negative response would not alter the assumption behind the question; either way, I would be saying that I read his mind.

A neon sign in the back of the barroom flashed on, and it was advertising a popular brand of beer. I don't remember the exact brand. The sign said Drink Brand X Beer. So he took a drink of his beer. And when the sign went off, he put his glass down.

Only, this time he put his glass down so hard that it shattered from the bottom up, right there in his hand, and flat beer spilled all over the table, and off the table, and on my shirt and in my lap.

It startled me and the beer was cold, so I jumped up involuntarily from my chair with a gasp. I certainly hadn't expected that.

He wasn't looking at me. Maybe he was beginning to believe in me for a moment. Maybe he was afraid I was real enough to burn out his eyes for spilling beer all over me. I don't know, but I do know that he was not looking at me, and wouldn't look at me. He just stared at the table. Maybe he was trying to understand what had just happened. Or maybe he was trying to decide if it had really happened at all.

It was not because I was upset that I decided at that point in time to leave the bar. But I couldn't really be expected to sit around in beer soaked shirt and shorts. So I went outside to stand around, and to get some fresh air. The air in the bar was stale.

Chapter
Twenty-Three

The air outside was hot.

I stood outside of the roadhouse watching my skin turn blue each time a LIQUOR sign flashed on, and I liked how the beer felt upon my clothes. It cooled me off. Someone walked by me and did not look at me or even notice me at all. He just wanted to go inside and get a beer.

Probably that man, whomever he was, didn't even believe I existed. Or anyone else, for that matter. Well, he had no reason to.

I guess my friend must have come out when the other man went in, because I had heard the door open only once, yet the next thing I knew my friend was standing nearby, and he was not drinking or smoking. He was just standing there. By the time I noticed him, he still had shown no sign of noticing me. He was just standing there, watching the sky and the road, rocking on his heels occasionally.

Although there were no clouds in the sky, he said It Looks Like Rain.

After he said this, I looked up at the sky and saw that there were no clouds in the sky, and that it did not at all look like rain. I don't remember my exact thoughts at that time, but I do remember thinking that his comment was odd and that it seemed inaccurate. This is how I know now that he had spoken magic words: it rained an hour later.

He said he'd buy me a beer, and that he was sorry about pouring beer all over my lap. He even stood before me to show that beer had spilled onto him, too.

I told him that I wasn't really in the mood for beer, and that I tried not to drink it too often because it was unhealthy and tended to dehydrate you. He said he'd buy me water with a twist of lemon in it, which is just about the best drink one can have on a hot day. More importantly, when someone asks you twice to be allowed to buy you a drink, then you know they really do want to buy you a drink or else they wouldn't have asked a second time. This in itself, after having spent quite a bit of time walking alone across the country, was like a drink of fresh lemon water on a hot day.

So I said yes.

He bought himself another beer, and he bought me a tall glass of ice water with a twist of lime, because they had run out of lemons. But lime is just as good. We took seats at the bar at first, but I couldn't think of anything to say, and neither could he. So then he said we should sit down, so we took a table, but the music was too loud. So then he said there was a place upstairs that he liked because it was peaceful there. He said the music and lights were bothering him. He said he'd show me the upper floor of the roadhouse.

I am not crazy, so I said I didn't want to see the upper floor of the roadhouse. I wasn't afraid of him, because at any given moment I could have easily defended myself with a mere glance. But when a strange man asks you to go into isolation with him, you tend to be a little suspicious, and I was. So I said I didn't want to go upstairs with him and thanks any way.

He showed me to the door of the stairway leading up, and he said I should come along, and was I afraid? No matter how hard I tried after that, I couldn't argue then, because I didn't want to say that I was afraid of something. So I said yes, and I followed him upstairs.

Chapter Twenty-Four

The upper room was small and obviously rarely used. There was no light in the room at all, but an entire wall was made of windows, so the LIQUOR signs outside provided light. There were a lot of boxes, full of things like napkins and toothpicks, and plastic cups, and such. I guess the bar used the room as storage space but they didn't organise it very well. There was a lot of dust, too, so lucky for me, I didn't have allergies. There was a comforting musky smell there, like an old castle or coal mine smells. The floor was uneven and weak. There was no carpet or furniture there.

He asked me if I thought the room was nice. I said I did not. He then clarified his question, explaining that he meant "nice" to mean "peaceful". To this, I agreed, because compared to the bar, it really was. And my lime water was refreshing, and it was relaxing me. It was brightening my day. He told me that he didn't believe I was real, and he told me that he didn't believe much of anything was real. At first I did not believe him. I thought he was just making up things to say, just for *fun*. But he meant what he said.

I told him that I did not believe it looked like rain. He told me that he thought it did. And we stood at the window and looked at the sky, and neither of us said anything, and we just stood there wondering whether it really would rain or not.

Of course it would. As I have said, it would rain in about an hour. But this I did not know at the time.

My friend told me that the room we were in was his favourite place in the roadhouse. He said it was peaceful there. We could still hear the music, faintly, through the floor. We heard a group of loud men enter the bar. We could hear their voices. We could hear them order their drinks, because they ordered loudly.

Chapter
Twenty-Four

We could hear them talk about the music, because they didn't like it and they wanted it changed but none of them wanted to spend the money on the jukebox because they barely had enough money for their drinks.

I had a premonition that they would end up in the very room in which me and my friend were standing in silence, drinking our drinks. They would come in and they would be surprised to see us there. And at first they would be silent, too, because me and my friend would be silent. But then they'd start talking again, and they'd be noisy, and they would be annoying, and it would eventually drive me and my friend back downstairs. But what would happen then, I had no idea about. I did not even think to wonder.

It was very dangerous for my friend at that time. He was ready to surrender. He was ready to give himself over to anyone. He no longer wanted to have to make his own choices, or to make decisions. He no longer wanted to feel like he was alive. He wanted to have his life determined by someone or something else, and he wanted to believe that they were making the right choices for him.

I have never seen anyone ready to surrender

      like he was.

I had never met anyone who really didn't believe that life was real enough to contend with. Usually people take life pretty seriously. Or if they don't take it seriously, at least they want to be in control of it. But my poor lost found friend didn't even want that much. He didn't take life seriously, he didn't feel like he could jump off, and he didn't want to be in control.

Or it could have been that everyone felt this way, and I just hadn't realised it until that point.

Chapter
Twenty-Four

So it is a good thing that I came along when I did. If it had been anyone else, my friend could have been in serious trouble. He might have come under the influence of someone really undesirable, or someone who is sick, or who would not consider my friend's best interest.

I could see from the start that my friend was in need of help. He needed to be rescued. He needed to be helped.

But I was not the person to help him.

I could not even remember my own name. Or my family's name. I was wandering across the country in the same pair of shorts and t-shirt, with my only possessions stuffed into my pockets.

I could not help him in the way he wanted to be helped. But I do believe that he is better now, because I did not help him. I did not want his troubles added to my life, so I drank my glass of lime water, and I stood in the attic storage room, and I listened to him talk when he decided to talk.

But I didn't once offer to help him.

And I think in this way that I may have saved him from a lot of confusion.

Most people once thought it was quite a special virtue to be helpful. They called it being a Good Samaritan, after a story about a man who helped a dying man who had been beaten, robbed, and left for dead on the side of the road. But no one really thought to ask whether there may have been a variety of different types of "help".

I have known for some time that helping a man who has been beaten, robbed, and left for dead is not at all the same thing as taking control of a man's life who has stopped believing that life was real. There are no grounds for comparison, in fact. These are two different concepts entirely.

My friend said: "I'm thinking about getting away from here. I'm thinking of leaving this all behind."

And he also said a few moments later: "Maybe I'll go South."

And then he said: "Or maybe I should just stay here and save up my money."

He wanted me to tell him what to do. But of course I said nothing.

He asked me what I was doing in the roadhouse. He told me he hadn't seen a woman in months. He told me mostly the area consisted of grumpy men who worked all day and got drunk at night. I told him I'd already noticed.

I said I was wandering around. I said I'd lost my car. I told him I didn't know where I was going.

He said No, Neither Do I.

He really said a mouthful in those few words.

We could hear by then the group of men who had entered earlier, the ones who had complained about the music. They were saying now that they didn't like the roadhouse, that they didn't like its atmosphere. They said can't a man get drunk in peace around here?

My premonition had been correct, and we could hear the group of men making their way up the stairs toward the upper room where we stood. We fell silent, because we both knew the men would come in, and we were none too excited about that. So we waited until the door opened, and then we looked at our drinks, and out the window, and at the floor, and didn't say anything.

The men remained in the doorway and they were silent, too. It was what could be called an awkward silence. And that is how it remained for about a minute, until the men entered the room quietly. One or two of them said "hi there" to us, and "How are you?"

We didn't respond. But we nodded a little.

The men stood around and sipped their drinks in silence. We all looked out the window as if we were entranced by some common element outside, but there was nothing to look at. I looked at my friend, and then back at the window, and then he looked at me, and then back at the window, and then I'd look at him again, and it would all happen over again. And the men from the bar kept looking over at me, because they did not trust me, because I'm a girl.

They started saying things to break up the silence. They said things like "Shit, what a night," and then they would all be silent again.

Then someone else would say, "Shit, what a day."

And they would all sip their drinks.

And finally someone would say, "Shit, what a life."

And they'd all agree.

Obviously none of them really had anything to say, so they were just saying things they felt were not inappropriate for the moment. This is practised by most everyone at some point in their life, but some people make a habit of it. Even I have on occasion fallen prey to the idea that no matter what, something must be said in moments of extended silence.

It does not matter if it is a large group or just two people: the lack of anything useful or sensible to say is not an acceptable excuse for not saying anything.

I seem to recall being in a bar once, some time ago, and I was not drinking because I did not want to gain weight. So in a way, I was the only one in the entire room, other than the bartender, who had my wits about me. Everyone else was drunk, including the two people with whom I was sharing a table. They were not chattering away drunkenly like you hear about. They were just sitting there with big smiles on their faces and glasses of liquor in front of them. They would not say anything. They just smiled.

But they were so uncomfortable with the silence that they kept telling me to say things. They demanded that I talk to them. I had to tell them all sorts of things, like how the Great Wall of China was built and that there were dead people built into the wall itself, and why the Taj Mahal was built, and how we know that aliens used the Pyramids of Giza as outposts for incoming UFOs.

I had no desire to tell them these things whatsoever. I just wanted to sit and drink the bottle of tea I'd bought from the convenience store next door. But they wouldn't let me. They made me speak. And like dogs or infants, they didn't care what was being said. They only wanted to see my lips moving and to hear my voice.

And when my lips moved and my voice made a sound, they smiled and smiled, wider and wider.

It doesn't take a drunk person to think someone speaking is entertaining. It's the general consensus, in fact. Sometimes people find themselves saying all sorts of interesting and surprising things just to avoid silence. They say things

like "Looks like it's going to be a windy day"

and "I saw something interesting on tv last night"

and "How's life treating you?"

and "Be mine"

and "I love you"

and other things they don't really mean.

The men from the bar eventually fell into conversation. A full, well rounded conversation. I don't remember exactly what they spoke about.

One asked my new friend if he was a worker around the area. My friend said that yes, he was. He was supposed to ask the same of them, but he didn't. He just said Yes I Am and then he didn't say anything else.

So the men told him about themselves any way.

I never ask to hear a Long Story. If I happen to ask someone a simple question for any reason, and they say Oh That's A Long Story, then I never persist for an answer. In fact, I try to avoid the answer. A Long Story is by nature full of more information than really needs to be revealed, and very boring.

These men gave us a Long Story about how they had come to arrive at that bar. They were not locally employed, but they had gained access to their boss's truck, which was company property. But their boss was away and he had left the keys to the truck unlocked, so they took the keys and they took the truck, and all night long they would be going from bar to bar to drink and make fools of themselves. And if anyone decided to report them by the license plate number, their boss would have to take all of the blame.

They liked that idea a lot.

They liked it so much that they all started talking at once about how their boss sure would be surprised when he heard that he'd been seen miles and miles away having drinks at every bar in the area. I guess they were counting on their boss not being intelligent enough to figure out what had really happened. Maybe they were right; they know their boss and I don't.

They had brought up a bowl of pretzels, and they passed it around the room, and soon it came to me, and one of them asked if I wanted some pretzels. I realised at that point that I was actually quite hungry, so I helped myself. I have never tasted such excellent pretzels, stale though they were. My friend joined me, and he ate quite a few pretzels, too. We were both famished. The men soon forgot all about us, and they talked and laughed and drank and stomped their feet and slapped their knees.

And so finally me and my friend decided to blow. We took the pretzels with us, and we went downstairs, completely unaware that it was already beginning to rain outside.

Well, I was unaware; whether my friend was or not, I cannot say.

Chapter Twenty-Five

By the time we reached the ground floor, the rain was already pouring from the sky. That is how quickly it occurred. The minute I realised what was happening, I put down my drink and my pretzels and ran to the door. I could not believe my eyes. It hadn't looked like rain before, but now it was raining, as if by magic. And there is nothing like a little rain to cool off a hot night.

I went right outside. I completely forgot myself. I just went right outside and stood in the rain, and danced in the rain, and enjoyed the cool water. My hair was dancing happily in the cool rain and my clothes were clinging to my skin; I must have been quite a sight.

I guess I really was, because my friend came outside, too, but he didn't stand in the rain like I did. He just stood on the porch of the roadhouse and watched me. He had a strangely passive look in his eyes when I finally stopped hopping around to look at him, and so I wondered what was going on in that head of his. He didn't seem to be looking at me, or at the rain. He seemed to be just looking at everything all at once. Like he was looking at a forest without taking notice of individual trees.

But until then, I was having too much fun in the rain to notice my friend. That rain really did cool me off, and it was a relief on my hot skin. I could almost feel steam coming off of me as the cool water met my hot flesh. I was kicking puddles and shaking my head and waving my arms. I felt like I'd been walking through the Sahara Desert and I'd finally found an oasis with water and mermaids and those things. I felt like a new girl.

Rain is better than just splashing water on your face or even taking a shower. It is all natural. It is more refreshing. There is a smell of ozone in the air when it rains, which is a stronger form of oxygen than what is normally found in the atmosphere. That sweet smell combined with the cool water that just magically falls from the sky is one of those little pleasures in life that really makes it all seem like a good idea after all.

Whether life was actually a good idea at all is another matter.

But rain sure makes it seem like it was.

I tilted my head back and opened my mouth and drank the rain. I rubbed my face and bathed in the rain. I kicked puddles and danced in the rain.

And then I noticed my friend staring out at the scene, and so I stopped, and I straightened up my clothes, and hoped nothing was showing through. I hadn't thought about the dangers of a wet t-shirt, but I don't think he really noticed. And even if he did, I looked good so maybe I don't mind so much.

Behind my friend, still in the bar, a crowd had gathered. They were all watching me. They thought I was drunk. They'd never seen a girl go crazy in the rain before. The bartender said "Someone should take her home to make sure she gets there alright."

But he wasn't really concerned for me. He was implying that someone should take the opportunity to fuck me, because he thought I wouldn't resist, because I was drunk. For that implication I would have burned his eyes out, but there were too many other men there. If I had done something irrational, they would have attacked me just out of gender loyalty. A girl can't blind a man in a room full of men and expect to come out alive. The best she could hope for is to take a few men down with her. But I preferred to live. It was raining, after all, so I was happy.

My friend and I walked along the road together without a word between us.

I wasn't really going his way, although I told him so when he asked. He thought I was heading for a hotel or a trailer. He thought I was staying in the area. He had no way of knowing that I was a girl who was traveling without a destination, and that I had no place to stay along the trip. He knew nothing about me. I knew very little about him. We were total strangers in the larger scheme of things.

Neither of us minded.

Everyone at the bar thought we were going away to go fuck, though.

The men who had come upstairs drove by us in their boss's truck, low to the ground, and they all shouted and laughed and whistled and made cat-calls. They knew I couldn't do anything to them. I couldn't focus on them to blind them, because they were driving by too quickly, and they were too far away any way. So they made cat-calls and laughed and just kept driving on down the roadway. I hope they slid on the water and crashed.

My friend told me to pay no attention to them. He told me that they were just being typical men, and that he hated typical men. He also mentioned that he did not believe in love.

     The night was high and lonely

an expression that makes as much sense as any

to describe the remoteness of two people

walking together down a long wet road in a gentle rain.

     We could see the sky glowing from a distant city.

     The clouds were lit up and they were moving

across the horizon labouriously.

We could almost feel

the Earth spinning

beneath our

feet.

His trailer home was sitting in the middle of a field off the road like a temple. Small and box-like, it shone in the moonlight and glistened in the rain. He did not expect me to follow him to the door.

He asked me where I was staying, and he invited me inside for a drink. He expected me to name a hotel or an ad-dress but of course I had no place to stay. And I was determined to sleep in his trailer home, because regardless of how much I loved the rain, I had no desire to sleep in it. But I did not tell him all of this because I did not want to make him nervous or seem like I was imposing upon him. I did not want him to know that I was planning to take advantage of his hospitality.

We dripped water all over his floor, but it was tile so it did not matter. His trailer was small and dim and scattershot. He probably hadn't cleaned it in a year. He told me he'd get me a towel to dry off with. He found two, and brought them both to me, and smelled them, and gave me the one that smelled the least.

I dried myself as much as I thought necessary and returned the towel. He put it away in the trailer's small bathroom. The pre-fabricated home's floor creaked and thumped as he walked, because it was hollow underneath. It sounded and felt like would give way any moment. I felt that he must be living on the edge, to live on such a floor; like he was taking his life into his own hands every time he got up from his sofa to get a drink from the kitchen.

The trailer home had been built in a factory years ago, and brought to the field on a big truck, and dropped onto the ground and left there to be rented by local workers. They don't make homes like that any more, but that was how his home was made.

He said it wasn't much but it didn't leak. He said he was a simple man and all he needed were four walls and a roof that didn't leak.

And then he thought about it for a while, and said come to think of it, I could probably even stand a leak.

Yes, he was a simple man, my friend.

Without asking me if I wanted one, he brought me a drink from the kitchen. It was a bottle of juice. I drank it.

As we drank, standing in his living room, we looked out the trailer's small fiberglass windows, speckled though they were with rain. And we stayed pretty quiet.

I had never met anyone before who honestly, really did not believe in so many things. It seems pretty much everyone you meet believes in at least Love. But not my host. Not my new friend. He still did not even believe in me.

He said he expected that probably he'd wake up in the morning and go into the kitchen and find my bottle of juice still there, unopened, undrunk.

He did not believe in Love because he had seen no firm evidence that proved its existence. This was not a random decision on his part. He had pondered it and researched it and thought it through.

There was a lot of talk about Love. It was supposed to be something very special that happened between a woman and a man, and it was, in its most ideal form, supposed to be eternal. Conveniently for those who spoke of it, Love could not be seen or heard or touched. Its causes could not be defined. In fact, even its symptoms varied from case to case.

No wonder my friend found the concept hard to believe in.

It was a half-baked notion

It was a myth that hadn't even been fully developed before its telling.

He believed there might be something called Love that had nothing to do with a woman and a man, but with society instead. It was a sort of political love, or a communal love. He believed this might exist because he himself felt no animosity toward the world. He was quite impassive toward the world. He assumes that the absence of animosity had a name, and he thought that name might be Love.

But that isn't the same thing, of course. That's just apathy. The love that people always talk about isn't apathy. It is something that was supposed to change one's life. It was supposed to change everything, and it was supposed to be eternal.

Once he had met a girl and they were friends, and one day when an awkward silence fell over them, he said I Love You, so she said I Love You Too. And so they had fallen in Love.

What had actually happened, he realised much later, was that they had both just grown accustomed to having one another around. If he had come home a year before that and found a lady there sitting on his sofa listening to old Elvis records, he would have flipped his lid. He wouldn't have known what to do, or why she was in his trailer playing his records. But after a year, it becomes commonplace, and you no longer panic. And that's called Love.

And ideally, if he came home to see that lady sitting on his sofa every day of every year, and this happened eternally, it could be said that Love is indeed eternal.

In fact, he would be so accustomed to seeing her there every day after work that if one day she didn't show up, he would probably be very disappointed. In fact, he might be so disappointed that he might even become depressed, and worried. And he might be so depressed and worried that he might even get angry. It has been known to happen before.

This is called Love. And it is eternal.

And it is nothing at all like what people make it out to be.

That is why my friend did not believe in Love as people talked about it. He believed that people often became accustomed to one another, and they even became dependent on each other. But time could solve dependence. The more time that the dependence has to develop, the more time that is required for it to go away.

I heard about an old man whose wife died of old age a long time ago. They had been married for seventy years. Maybe more. Next thing anyone knows, the old man himself died. People were really upset. They had just finished burying his wife, and now they had to bury him. So they all stood around and said that he'd died of a broken heart.

It isn't true. He had died because for seventy years he had grown accustomed to having his old lady around, so it would have taken another seventy years for him to get her off his mind. But the old man was ninety years old and he didn't have seventy years to forget about her. So he died because his life was pretty much over any way. There was no use in waiting around, because he wouldn't last the seventy years it would take for him to forget about her.

And besides that, how could the same Eternal Love that everyone talks about being so great and wonderful and healing be the direct cause of someone's death?

It is a clear contradiction.

I believed, and still do believe, in Love, in spite of my friend's opinion. I know that Love on an interpersonal level does exist, although I concede that it is much rarer than is generally believed.

People talk about Love like it happens every day, some times even at first sight. In truth, it rarely happens at all. People desire something, and then they acquire it, and then they grow accustomed to having it. That's the truth behind the myth.

But not me.

I know I am in love because I never reached the final stage.

I desired Arthur P. Thomas, Jr. (my first and only true love), and I acquired his love, but he of course gave up the ghost before I could ever grow accustomed to him.

Yet I still am in love with him.

So it can't be argued logically that I don't really love him, and that I am just accustomed to him, because he no longer physically exists. Logically, I should have stopped loving him once he was gone. Or at the most a year or two thereafter, since we were together for such a short amount of time. I should have been able to find someone else. I should have, in my youthful exuberance, been able to find, through common and simple flirtation, someone else to love.

But I did not, and have not.

I haven't even had the desire.

I still do flirt. It is enjoyable to flirt. I could be accused of flirting with my old friend Richard C. Brown, and they would be right. Swimming in lakes completely nude constitutes flirtation. But I could not be rightly accused of falling in love with him.

I expect my love for Arthur P. Thomas, Jr. to be eternal. I expect to see him in Heaven, as a ghost. I expect we'll be very happy

dead.

He does not now realise that what I did to him was all for love, but that will be the first thing I say to him when I meet him in Heaven. I have made this resolution. I will not even bother saying Hello. I will just walk right up to him and explain that I did it all for love, and he will believe me, because you can't lie in Heaven.

In a way my friend and I had both lost interest in love. He had lost interest because he did not believe that it existed, and so he didn't waste time looking for it like most people do. And I'd lost interest in looking for love because I was already in love with someone, who happens to be dead at the time, and so I wasn't interested in looking for someone to love, even though I did believe it existed for me, at least.

Chapter Twenty-Six

It was not love that killed Arthur P. Thomas, Jr., though it may seem that way, if only indirectly. But it was not.

It was lack of proper communication.

Which was also a problem that my friend and I experienced. Either because he did not believe that I existed or because he was just bad at communicating, I don't think either of us really understood the other.

He told me to take a seat, and he cleared off a chair. I thought he was clearing it off for me, so I sat down in it when he turned to set aside the old laundry that had occupied the chair. When he turned back and saw me sitting there, I could tell from his expression that he had intended the seat to become his own.

But he was graceful and recovered quickly, and took a seat on the sofa. And he sighed and coughed and crossed his legs and moved from seat to seat on the sofa until finally he just laid down and put his cool drink to his forehead. It was as if though he had completely forgotten that I was there.

Which shouldn't have surprised me

since he did not believe I was there

    at all.

The next thing I knew, he was sound asleep.

So I sighed and coughed and crossed my legs and stomped my feet but nothing awakened him.

His belongings were few and simple. He had an old record player that looked about ready to fall apart. It looked like it might just shake into pieces if the volume was turned up too loud.

His records were all scratched and worn. He listened to old music, like Elvis and Bob Marley and The Tijuana Brass and Henry Mancini.

There was one more room in his small home, which was his bedroom. In total, there were three rooms. There was the kitchen, the living room, and the bedroom, and then there was the bathroom. The bathroom was almost a closet. It did not even have a bathtub, only a shower.

I went into his bedroom to have a look around. I could not resist looking around while he slept. It seemed like the appropriate thing to do. I wanted to search through his home and find out more about him. I wanted to poke through his things but not be obtrusive. It was that natural curiosity that I think everyone feels about a strange environment.

In his bedroom there was a closet, a chest of drawers, and his bed. On his bed were his clothes, and his closet was almost empty. I found that amusing even then.

I took a seat on his bed and opened the chest of drawers, one drawer at a time. There wasn't much there to see. There were socks, and boxer shorts, and T-shirts. In other drawers there were old paperback novels by any given variety of dime speculative-fiction authors. There were a lot of classics there. In other drawers there were just odds and ends, like scissors and bits of twine and spare change and matchbooks and local maps.

And in the top drawer on the right-hand side of the drawer there were old letters and photographs. The photographs were as old and worn as his records in the other room, but these were decades more recent. There was a girl's face in the photographs, and she was dark-skinned and had beautiful brown-red snakes for hair, and beautiful and wide eyes that made me feel poetic, and say things like "Her eyes make me think of onyx stones." I would say that later, of course, because at the time I was alone and had no one to whom I could speak.

The letters were long and nervous, and not well written. I could tell the writers were unsure of themselves. They were not sure if they should be writing at all, and even less sure of what they were saying. They were nervous confessions.

The sentences were carefully constructed so that they did not say too much but suggested everything. It was familiar to me because I know how to flirt, too.

There were letters from a lady, and letters from my friend back to her. All were handwritten, and the ink was fading from age. Most everything fades from age.

I did not read them all. I could not bring myself to. I read one or two letters, and then parts of three or four more. I read them because I was curious. I am not always curious by nature, but of my new friend, I was.

It seems he'd been loved before, but the man in those letters seemed a complete stranger to me. Like it had been another lifetime, although I don't believe in transmigration of soul. But I do believe in life after death, since I know of a few people who have died and are still alive now. Actually I know of one such person, but probably there have been more.

For all I know, my friend is one of them.

It certainly seemed like it to me

      from reading those letters.

For one thing, the man in the letters was happy.

And for another, he believed in a lot of things.

The man asleep on the old sofa in the next room did not so much as believe the sun would rise in the morning. Much less did he believe in calling a woman "my beautiful flower" like the man in the letters did.

I would have liked to be called a beautiful flower by someone, although it's an awfully silly thing to say. It sounds poetic, though, and most everyone likes poetry from time to time.

In fact I have met many people of many different types, and they all end up surprising me when they look at a colourful sunset and say things like "I feel the sky has been painted by some great ghost, like da Vinci's, or Monet's." Or when they see a little kitten and start talking to it like it was their own child.

I met a man who must have weighed three-hundred pounds, and he was tall and muscular, and I thought he would be very intimidating. And in fact, he was. Because he worked at a bar as a bouncer, which is someone whose job it is to physically abuse disruptive drunkards, because for some reason bar owners just couldn't figure out where all those disruptive drunkards were coming from. So he was well respected if not feared. I was a little intimidated by him myself, that much is certain.

Imagine my surprise when he started talking to me about his favourite book of all time: Alice In Wonderland, which he found astoundingly charming and full of imagination.

And there was a very cynical pessimist who I met, who always said the world was better off dead, and that most people were too stupid to deserve to live. He expected fascism to take over, which it hasn't, or for the world to just suddenly fall apart at the seams, which it hasn't. And when anyone spoke of love, he just laughed, and he also scorned pity.

Chapter
Twenty-Six

All in all, one might say that he was a pragmatist. But when someone said that they would like to watch a sunset with him, he was sure to show up early. One thing he didn't say was that he doubted the sun would set.

I've met all sorts of people, and even the ones that were openly rude and mean and cruel and hostile could be caught off guard at some point, during which time I could sometimes read their minds, which is a trick I had taught myself as a child, and I found that they would be thinking about how much they loved a good stroll in the woods and hearing birds sing.

It seems everyone has some kind of ideal that they hold high above everything else. It may not be something that is shared by others in great numbers, but it's a poetic ideal.

Ideals are things that are usually unrealistic by nature. For example, the Communist Ideal as set forth long ago by two very famous writers named Mr. Karl Marx and Mr. Engels, whose first name no one knows, was that everyone in society should share everything equally without the imposition of a governing class.

This of course was never realised.

It is also a popular religious ideal.

The ideal for a society that was ruled by the people and gave an equal chance to everyone to achieve their personal goals whether or not those goals were compatible with anyone else's was set forth by Mr. Thomas Jefferson, whose head you will see on any old silver nickel, and many other rich white men.

This obviously was never realised either.

Just about the only ideal that has come about so far is the ideal of anarchy, and it has rather happened by accident. If it has in fact happened at all. The thing about anarchy is that there's no one around to make it official. So possibly no one will ever realise that it exists, or if someone does then no one else will agree.

Like everyone else on this planet, I also have a poetic ideal that keeps me smiling when there is nothing to otherwise smile about. It is the picture of me living on a beach somewhere, in a house, alone, with maybe just one friend who may stop by when we get bored. That comes to mind when I get in the mood to think of poetic ideals.

And it keeps me happy sometimes.

Probably it doesn't really need to be said, but after I read those old letters, I began to see my new friend in a new light.

I thought that maybe if I'd kept photographs and letters, then perhaps I'd remember things better. But I still might not believe in them. In a way I guess my friend had turned his entire old lifetime into a poetic ideal, and then stopped believing in poetic ideals altogether.

Now, that's really doing something. When you have done something like that, you really know you've done something big.

I hadn't heard my friend stir, but he had gotten off of his old dusty sofa and he'd gone into the small bathroom to shave. I don't know what prompted him to get up and shave at such an hour, but that is exactly what he did. It was the first thing he did after he awakened.

I became aware of his activity only after I'd finished reading some of his letters. And then I continued looking through his photographs. I listened to the water running in the shallow sink, and the razor tap and splash into the water there.

He entered the room with shaving cream still on parts of his face, and he was holding the dripping wet razor in his hand, and over his shoulder was his towel. He stood in the doorway for a few moments, and then he sat down on the bed next to me. The mattress bounced and shook and squeaked, but it did not fall down.

He looked over my shoulder at the photographs. And he saw the love letters, opened and out of order, on the chest of drawers before us. For a moment I thought he might be angry, although I did not fear him. I just felt sorry for him, whether he got mad or not.

I didn't think it would be right for him to get angry about his former lifetime. I thought it would be better for him, and better for the memories themselves, for him to remain calm. An outburst then would ruin everything. It would make his former lifetime really disappear.

But all he did was sit there, looking at the photographs in my hand. And as I glanced at each new photograph,

one at a time,

so did he,

one at a time.

When he'd seen all the photographs and made no further comments than the obvious one about the lady's hair, he sat back and took a deep breath. He put the razor down next to the old love letters but did not touch them.

I could smell his shaving cream, cheap and fading from his face, and I think he'd forgotten about it.

Then he reached forward and held the letters in his hands. He said "I remember these" which I thought was such an unusual thing to say, because of course he remembered them; he'd clearly read through them every night. But he really seemed to be speaking honestly, like every day he forgot about the letters until he opened the drawer in which he kept them, and then he remembered everything.

There may be such a drawer for everyone.

Even for me.

Chapter Twenty-Seven

He stroked his chin and said he remembered.

That is when I said that her eyes made me think of onyx stones.

He said she'd had the most beautiful red in her hair. He said he didn't know where that had come from, but somehow her hair was slightly red. And he was not making this up; I could see her red snakes in the photographs.

That is the wonderful thing about eyes: they are almost always beautiful. No matter when they are seen, they are nice to look at, and to gaze into. And with the right person you could see magical things.

With Arthur P. Thomas, Jr., for example, I used to see the stars in his eyes, because he was always laying on the grass staring into he sky. So it was common to see the Milky Way reflected in his big brown eyes.

Yes, Arthur P. Thomas, Jr. had big brown eyes.

I asked my friend what he used to see in the woman's onyx stone eyes.

He said he could remember seeing the treetops in her eyes. He said there was always the blue sky and the very tops of trees in those eyes, like he was a butterfly dancing in the breeze just above a mysterious enchanted forest.

He said there were rainbows in those eyes.

If the light caught them right.

It was then that I knew that before I died, I would be confronted with two eyes that reflected the beach in them. Just like my poetic ideal. I would see a beach, with a nice white house, and a gray blue sky. The beach of my fantasies is not bright and sunny and hot, but cool and windy and tumultuous.

He said he didn't think of those photographs often. I don't know if I believe him. I didn't at the time. I thought at the time that maybe he did think of them, only he didn't know he did.

It is my opinion that it is better to dream abut the past than complain helplessly about the present. I have heard a lot of people complain about their present situation, whatever it may be, but they cannot seem to do anything about it, so all they do is talk themselves in circles. But when they are talking about the past, they just talk happily about the good old days, and then they fall silent and just sit around with a pleasant smile on their face, remembering even more that they don't want to say out loud. In fact, they sometimes find that sitting in silence with that pleasant smile helps them remember, because they don't have to concentrate on speaking.

And that is what my friends did: he fell silent and just smiled pleasantly and remembered. Then he stood up and went to his mirror and rubbed some hair cream into his hands, and ran his hands through his hair until it shone.

He said he used to live out west. He said it was warm where he'd lived, which pretty much goes without saying, actually. But he said it anyway. He said if he could have anything at all that he wanted in the known or unknown universe, he would want to be back there, with her.

He said he would do anything to be with her again. And that cameras should be banned from the face of the planet. With that, he went back into the living room and into the little closet bathroom to finish shaving.

I followed him. As he shaved, I watched. He must have felt self-conscious, because he closed the door in my face. I waited on the sofa.

When he came out, he looked somewhat refreshed. He said We All Have Our Favourite Tragic Memories. He was trying to belittle his own grief, or his own memories. I could tell. He did not actually believe what he was saying, but he wanted to. He needed to believe his sense of tragedy was unimportant to everyone, including himself.

Unfortunately for him, he had met the one person in the world who could honestly disagree with him. He had met me.

Unlike other people, who might disagree with him just to be antagonistic, or else to make him feel better, I could actually say truthfully that I did not have my own Tragic Memory. I would not be making that up. I would be telling the truth.

And so that is what I told him. I told him

Not Me.

He laughed spitefully. It was clear that he did not believe me yet.

So I told him truthfully that I had no memory. I told him I did not even remember my own name with any amount of certainty. I told him that I vaguely remembered killing a few people, and I remembered a soda fountain back home in my youth. But all in all I had no significant amount or recollection of my past. And even the bad memories I do have are not tragic; they are just moments in the past.

The death of my one and only true love, Arthur P. Thomas, Jr., was a terrible thing, but it is not a Favourite Tragedy. it is something that happened long ago, and something that will be explained away after death. It is not something I try to prevent by sitting around in the present and thinking about it all day.

That is a Favourite Tragedy: something that someone thinks about so intensely and so often that they forsake the present for the memory. I will comment on this more later.

There is an old saying:

> *In a few years, we'll look back at all of this and laugh.*

It is meant to be comforting idea, implying that current tragedies don't really matter in the longer scheme of one's lifetime. It's nonsense, of course, since everything in life necessarily affects life. But the idea that few things are so important that they threaten life itself sometimes can be comforting. It makes life seem to have a meaning. Other times it can be depressing, because it also makes life seem insignificant and meaningless.

For instance, my friend was not looking back at his former life and laughing. He was looking at his present life and laughing at it. And in a sense, I think I was, at the time, looking at my future and laughing. Why else would I be walking across country without knowing exactly where I was going?

He asked me why I had no memory of my past, and I told him honestly that I did not know. He told me it wasn't normal to have no memory. He added that even so, he wouldn't have minded having that same problem.

He said when he earned enough money maybe he'd move away. He said maybe he'd Start Over. It is popularly believed that changing one's physical location is a valid way of starting life over with a fresh start.

Physical travel, it seems, is a metaphor for mental progress.

Maybe that is why I travel.

I was fairly certain that I was hearing him correctly when he said that Time Heals All Wounds, and so I agreed.

Neither of us had much money.

I once saw a man with money. He had more money than he knew what to do with. Was he happy?

Yes, in fact, he was.

He had nothing to worry about because he could buy the solution to most anything. So he was the happiest man alive.

Was his life spiritually satisfying?

Again, yes it was. By his own definition, which is the only one that counts to someone, really, his life was full and satisfying.

Some people say money doesn't matter and that money isn't important. But they are wrong. Money is all that matters in an environment built around Money. What people are really saying when they say money isn't important is that the World Doesn't Matter. Since the world is built around Money, then they are also saying that Money Doesn't Matter. They are saying you should reject the world, and you will just happen to reject money along with it because money is so important in the world. It seems like a fine distinction, but it is not just semantics.

The world is based on money just as always. It always will be, probably. Or it might not, which would surprise me.

To reject money is to reject the world. To reject money is to say that its religion, which is the religion of money, is not a valid force in your life. I guess I have kind of rejected the world. I guess a lot of people have. I know my friend has, since he doesn't even believe it exists.

But for the people who are still excited about the world, money is a really hot commodity. It lets them do things like eat, drink, sleep, and wear clothes. Also, it is good for things like drugs, sex, and rock n' roll. It is good for *fun*. And it buys things like cars and televisions and boats and games and purebred pets and collectable trinkets and jewelry and guns and dozens of suits-and-ties and shoes. And it repairs or replaces these things once they have become worn down at the end of each month. It makes them happy and solves all of the problems in their world. And it makes them really feel like they are a part of the world, so they know they exist, since they believe the world exists.

The only complication happens when someone stops believing in the world. Then money can't make them happy.

Lucky for my friend, he didn't believe in the world. I guess I still did because I often imagined winning a million dollars, which is pretty much a confession to believing in the world.

I know so much about this because I pay attention to things most people don't really notice. I am not a professional. I have not done an in-depth study of this. But I know that most people who consciously reject the world are the people with a religion other than money. These are called non-monetary religions. There are exceptions even within each religion, but the pure, ideal forms are non-monetary -- even if only in theory. There are always those poetic ideals.

I realised this when I was handed a Bible on the street once. You can't walk down a city street without being handed a Bible or a Koran. Not so much outside of the cities though. I wanted to pay the woman for the Bible but she wouldn't take any money.

She had a box full of Bibles and she was giving them away to everyone who passed by, for free.

If money was really important, you wouldn't get Bibles and Korans for free.

Somewhere, somehow, someone prints up tiny little Bibles and Korans and I Chings and sends them to people to be given away. You will sometimes find normal size Bibles and Korans being given away because a warehouse is clearing out stock and generally people don't buy books much. But usually you get those small Bibles and Korans and I Chings made especially to be given away for free. They don't even bother putting a price or a bar code on these books because they aren't being made to be sold and everyone involved knows it. They are being made to be given away for free.

I do not know how it is possible to fit so much into one small book that will fit into your pocket.

I usually end up giving my free books away. I can't seem to hold onto them. I am always giving them to someone else for free. And then they think I am a fanatic and will try to convert them or make them say magic words to save their soul. But I'm not, and I don't.

Chapter Twenty-Eight

A certain amount of uncertainty comes along with every new day a person finds herself facing. There is no way to avoid this.

> An argument playfully lost
>
> a joke badly told
>
> a pleasure begrudgingly denied.
>
> It is clear
>
> that people have no idea
>
> as to what they want.

My friend knew what he wanted, and that is rare even now, but he suffered for it, because the one thing he really wanted was just not possible, and there was nothing he or anyone else could do about it. Except perhaps Dr. Patricia R. Durham, who can do just about anything that can be done. The problem was, of course, that this just couldn't be done, maybe not even by the great Dr. Patricia R. Durham. Even she has her limits, and she will be the first to tell you so.

`"I'm not God, and I wouldn't want to be, either."

• Dr. Patricia R. Durham

Sometimes I think it may be best for people not to know what they want, because at least in not knowing, neither are they aware of the futility of their goals.

Lucky for me, I had no goals.

I did not even know the name of the state I was in at the time, much less what I wanted out of life. If there even were states any more. Possibly the concept of statehood had dissolved by that time.

I remember clearly at that point that I realised very suddenly: I had no idea about what my age was.

I had forgotten my own age.

I could remember the date of my birthday but I could not recall how many I'd had. I had a general idea, and still do, but I could not remember a specific age.

If you do not think about it often, you sometimes forget small details like that. If I'd been asked, or if I am asked, I can give an approximation, but only within two or three years, I think, of my actual age.

I asked my friend if he could remember his age. He said he had stopped keeping track of birthdays after he'd hit thirty. He must have been a lot older than me. He didn't look old, just worn out. Like he'd been spent, and now he was just waiting around to be taken away. He looked as if he'd lived his life already, but just happened not to have died yet.

I used to think I'd had a pretty full life, but looking at my friend, I knew that I had only just begun. And I was glad for it. I would rather be young and inexperienced than young and all used up.

A lot of people you meet will say to learn from elders. They make this an unqualified statement, meaning that they put no conditions on it or make an attempt to prove it. They just accept it and expect everyone to accept it. But what they don't realise is that some older people never learned from themselves, and that is no kind of person to learn from. Except in the reverse, maybe; one might learn what not to do. So maybe people are right to say to learn from elders. But I still don't think so.

I have learned nothing from my friend, although I value his friendship. Any time someone tries to be a friend, you know there is sincerity there. Even if they are just sincerely lonely and just need someone to talk to, it is significant that they are making the effort to contact someone.

Making any kind of contact with someone is in a way a proof of existence. It is verifying that the person is real, and that you are real. Although my friend didn't, and still doesn't, believe that I exist, at least he made the effort. That was an important thing.

Sometimes if you are walking down a street and no one looks at you and no one says anything out loud, and everyone is just passing by like no one else exists, you actually start to question if you are really there. I have seen people ponder this, and sometimes they jump out in front of cars just to see if they will stop. If they stop, they assume they exist.

So human contact is not just a way to end boredom, although it may be that, too. A lot of people will talk to someone else just because they are bored and can think of nothing better to do. They will talk and talk even if they have nothing really to say.

It is also a way to make sure we all exist. If you are talking to someone, and they are responding, you feel like you are both really there and that you both really exist. It isn't true, but it seems true. People talk to people who don't exist all of the time.

It is what my friend thought he was doing when he spoke to me.

For all I know, he still talks to me day in and day out.

I saw a man in a business suit walking down a busy street one day, and he looked very stable and reasonable and rich, and he was just talking away and shaking and nodding his head and throwing his hands into the air, and there as no one with him. He was having a very intense conversation with either himself, or a ghost, or a completely imagined person. Or possibly he was speaking with God.

It made me wonder what his respectable companions Back At The Office thought of him. I guess he talked to himself there, too. Some crazy people sneak through life without being caught. They have charm or money. Or creativity. If they are creative then they are called eccentric, unless they cut off their ear and send it to a girlfriend (which is a true story, and actually happened). Then they are called crazy.

But when one has money, one can talk to anyone one wants to, even people who don't really exist. Some day someone might notice that crazy businessman chattering away to himself, and then everyone will see that he's crazy, but probably not. I don't think anyone actually cares.

That businessman was assuring himself that both he and his imaginary companion existed by establishing human contact with that imaginary person. So I'll bet he was feeling pretty proud of being real. But little does he know that his companion does not exist. So much for human contact proving existence. And since you have no way of knowing if that businessman exists, since I could have just made the whole story up as an elaborate lie, I guess the fact that he was talking even to himself proves nothing. Insofar as anyone else but me is concerned, that businessman only has a 50% chance of actually being real, and a 50% chance of being as imaginary as his nonexistent companion. Only I know if I really saw him out on the street that day or if I just made him up in my mind as a good story to tell.

And even if I did see it, even that might have been a hallucination.

Chattering constantly either intelligently or otherwise is not proof of existing.

The way is clear: either everything exists or nothing exists. Put another way: either it all exists or none of it exists. By this it is meant that either that businessman and his imaginary friend exists, or neither of them exist. The imaginary friend can't be nonexistent and the businessman be existent. It is both or neither.

I believe that.

I believe this because as I've said, there is no way to prove that the businessman is any more existent than his imaginary friend. To me, and to everyone else, there are equal chances for both that they existed or not.

For us to say that one exists and the other does not, 100% proof would have to be established for one, and 100% proof against the other.

But so far 50% for each is the best anyone can do. So it has to be admitted that they are equal. So either both do exist, or both don't exist.

My friend would say it all doesn't exist. This isn't really nihilistic of him. It is just what he believes.

Me, I prefer to believe it all exists.

I believe that ghosts exist, for example, even though I have met one or two people who do not. If I did not believe in ghosts then I would have to stop believing in Arthur P. Thomas, Jr. And if I ever stop believing in him, I may as well just stop believing in myself.

It's all or none, and that is how I see it.

Just because someone is imaginary or dead or hasn't been born or even conceived yet doesn't really mean they don't exist. It just means they are at different stages of existence than the average joe.

I consider myself pretty much just an average joe. I have not really done anything very spectacular in my life yet. I do not look Spent, or worn out, like my friend does. I am just like many other people. I am just trying to get through life without being bothered too much by other people, but not so ignored by them so that I feel lonely.

Everyone gets lonely eventually. This is something that God in Infinite Wisdom built into the human psyche. Even hermits start to get lonely, so they make friends with birds and ladybugs and things of that nature. Saint Francis of Assisi, a very spiritual man who lived very long ago, was lonely, and so he started talking to animals, and they could even understand him. That is another true story and it is why there are animals in Heaven. Muhammad was so friendly to animals that when he was hiding in the cave, a group of spiders built a web over the entrance so no one would find the great holy man as he hid from them. They wanted to kill him. They wanted to kill a man who had talked to Gabriel. It is why you will never see a Moslem kill a spider.

You will never see me kill a spider, either.

Chapter Twenty-Nine

Sleep is like death.

so I avoided it.

When you are comfortable in bed, sometimes it feels like you are in a coffin. Especially when you stare up at the dark formless ceiling of the room, and all around it is completely silent.

Sometimes walking down a lonely road at night, you feel like a ghost wandering the Earth, trying to find your way home. And I should know, because I've walked that road before.

I don't know exactly what it feels like to be a ghost, but I imagine it must be very lonely, although there are probably more ghosts than there are live people, considering that this Earth has had such a long history. Although we may never know for sure, no matter how hard scientists try to find out, because the one thing they can't do is take a population count of souls.

These days, that's about the only thing scientists can't do.

I have a feeling my friend must have felt that way every day, and I guess he didn't sleep much either, or if he did he enjoyed it more than being awake.

No one knows exactly what sleep is. It is the closest thing we will come to death and still live. A lot of people see ghosts and angels, and even God, in their sleep. And they get answers to questions in dreams. So it is obvious why sleep can be dangerous.

Still, it is necessary to sleep, and so everyone does it.

Sleep is a little death.

Dreams are a little heaven.

or hell.

Sometimes people don't even want to wake up, so good are their dreams. Other times people awaken screaming and in a cold sweat because they have had such a terrifying nightmare.

And when I dream

I dream I am alive.

Most everyone does.

But my friend, as he sat on his coffee table near me, said he preferred not to dream at all. He liked to sleep a deep sleep, totally unaware of anything. If he dreamt, then it seemed like he was awake, so there didn't seem like there was much of a point to sleeping. He said dreaming cheated a person out of unconsciousness.

So do those magical little poetic ideals, sometimes.

Sometimes things happen that seem like they are dreams, but they have really actually happened in real life. That is how life is. Sometimes dreams seem so real that they are mistaken for life, and other times life is so unusually odd or pleasant or terrifying that it seems like a dream.

A woman in the Northeast had witnessed her husband's death at an abandoned factory. They had gone there out of curiosity; they just wanted to see what the old dead factory was like. So they went inside for a tour. And unwisely, her husband had decided to take a shortcut through one of the machines he thought was dead, but he soon found that there was a little bit of life left in that factory yet, and with its last spark of life it compacted him into an eight-inch by eight-inch block of flesh and bone, as his wife stood watching in terror. She was helpless. She couldn't do anything.

Some people saw the couple's car on the side of the road. Eventually someone was curious enough to investigate. When they found the woman she was in a state of shock. So they hospitalised her, and examined her, and the medical people noticed that one of her arms was badly bruised. Blood vessels had actually ruptured in her arm. They asked her what part of the factory had attacked her to leave her with such an injury. They wanted to know how it had happened.

She told them.

She had pinched herself again

and again

     and again,

convinced that it was all just a bad dream, trying to wake herself up.

The bruise, rumour has it, never went away.

I believe it.

Of course the opposite may hold true for people of a suspicious nature. I know sometimes I doubt things that seem to be, as the saying goes, *Too Good To Be True*.

If my friend's long lost love suddenly returned to him, he would probably not believe it. He would say it was *Too Good To Be True*, and pinch himself again

and again

and again...

And then he'd enjoy it while is lasted, because that's the kind of person he is. He wouldn't spend too much time contemplating, he would just accept it, unreal or not.

Probably most of us would, in his place.

I like the moments in life that seem to be unreal. That is what I live for. Anything simple but unusual makes my day brighter. One day I was on a subway and a man sat down next to me wearily, saying under his breath El Haim Dulillah. Although I do not speak Arabic, I knew what the expression meant, so I said Thanks Be To God. And then the man said he was from Nigeria, and made three loud popping sounds with his hands, and said no more.

At the next station, he got off the train without a word.

Why he told me he was from Nigeria, and how he made those popping sounds, or why, I will never know. It was such a simple but unusual even that I honestly wondered for days afterwards whether my mind hadn't just wandered for a few moments and I'd imagined it. But as far as I know, it really did happen, and that's life, no doubt about it.

Sometimes, or most of the time, dreams or imaginings are preferable to what is "really" happening. It is why people love to be entertained. They forget about their real life, and so they become happy.

They become *Happy Campers*.

Whenever someone says to me that they are *Happy Campers*, I become suspicious, because usually that means that they have deluded themselves into believing *everything is OK* and that life is entertaining.

Some people believe they are *Happy Campers* for years and years until finally one day they wake up and realise that they are not happy at all, and have not been happy all that time after all.

What a way to start the day that would be. No amount of morning coffee, I suspect, could make you recover from discovering that the feeling you'd thought was contentment was actually just numbness, after all.

coffee.............................75¢

Here is a question which I did not make up. A bum, in search of enough change for a cup of coffee, actually asked me this question:

> *How can someone be naïve and yet not-stupid*
> *to the world?*
>
> — Randy

He said his name was Randy, and that in reality he had tangerine coloured skin. In spite of all empirical evidence to the contrary, I believed him. And I still do.

I gave him 75 cents so he could buy himself a cup of coffee.

And I give him full credit for his koan.

I thought at first that it was just a silly paradox that only sounded like it might be profound. But in actuality it is as profound as it sounds, and I guess when one is a bum and has no job, one has plenty of time to come up with profound questions like that.

I think many people are naïve in some ways, but they have lived for so long that they have learned to fake their way through the world by doing what they know the world expects of them, and so they might be said to be not-stupid to the world. But they are still tragically naïve.

Chapter
Twenty-Nine

No wonder people love to sleep.

And it's no wonder they like a pleasant dream.

Chapter Thirty

I've never minded a pleasant daydream, so I do daydream often. It is a common practise. My mind is always active. If I am not pondering life itself, I am pondering what life could be in an ideal situation.

When you are a writer, your mind must be always active.

When I told this to my friend that night, he said he believed me, and that I seemed like a ponderous person. He said I seemed like I must think a lot because I didn't talk much, but neither did I seem to be stupid. So he assumed something was going on in my head during my silence.

In truth, I could say the same of my friend. Because he didn't say much either, but I could tell that he was nobody's fool. His was that sort of silence that really suggested something was going on behind it. (And not always something good or healthy.)

Silence suggested to people the idea of being alone. They assumed that if someone is quiet and doesn't say much then that person must want to be alone, or else they would take advantage of having someone around, and speak. To a degree, this is true.

So people who are silent must like to be alone. And they sit around and say nothing, apparently quite content with just considering their own private thoughts, and they sleep, and dream their life away.

Well just look at my friend, who didn't even believe anyone else in the wold existed. That is isolationist if anything is.

And look at a girl walking across country, still in love with someone who is dead.

Those two people must want to be alone.

But actually I have no desire to be entirely alone. I wish to be left in peace, but that is not always the same thing as being left alone.

In fact, it was not until later that I realised that people have no desire to be lonely, yet some people simply do not know how to be with other people. They don't want to be lonely but cannot adjust to being not alone.

And so it came to pass:

I left my friend alone in his trailer with his old photographs

of his love who was probably dead,

or who just couldn't make him adjust to being

not alone.

There was no reason to stay with my friend because although I thought he was interesting and intriguingly strange, I simply did not exist in his world.

It was no accident that I had met my friend and that I went to his trailer and saw his photographs. I had gone there for a reason, although no one but God knew what it was.

But now I know, too, although I do not claim to be God. I know because I can see things like this in retrospect. You realise when you look back that some things just had to happen in life so that you could reach a certain point later on. For instance, without losing every penny that she owned, a lady might never become an assistant to the late greatest genetic scientist in the universe, and then she might never become the greatest scientist alive. Of course, I refer to the great Dr. Patricia R. Durham in this example.

As for me, I am no scientist and I am not famous. But I did meet someone who knew who I was, although I did not know who he was. And if I hadn't gone to my friend's trailer that night, I would have kept traveling, and the man who spoke to me would have never saw me and would have never had the chance to speak to me. It was his words that compelled me to hurry to the west coast of this nation, and to seek out the greatest living mind in the whole world.

I was to seek out the great Dr. Patricia R. Durham herself.

I do not know nor have I ever believed in coincidence. I think that the idea of coincidences was invented by someone who was too afraid of what an event suggested, and so she called it a "coincidence" and dismissed it. Probably she is dead by now. Probably her obituary says she died of a coincidence.

I never ignore things that appear to be coincidental. In fact, the more coincidental they seem, the more I tend to notice them. In fact, I would go so far as to say that the more coincidental something seems, then probably that is all the more deliberate. But I can say this for such things: no person on this whole planet can really account for coincidences. They cannot explain them and they cannot prevent them. They are just something people have to live with, like miracles, and science, and other things that cannot be explained.

So I would not say that I had met my friend by mere chance. I would say that we were meant to meet, and it was meant to rain, and I was meant to go inside his little trailer home, and to ultimately leave him there as disillusioned as when I first met him hours before.

And all this was just to lead up to that man in the street who, when he recognised me, called me not by name but in a very formal manner, and told me that there was a place on the west coast of the nation. He said that I had to go there before there was no west coast of that nation

because things were happening

and they were happening fast

and soon there wouldn't be much left of any of us.

The man was a raving lunatic.

But what he said was true, and that was something I will never forget. The fact is that for a week my life found direction because of that raving lunatic.

I do not know if the man was clinically insane, which is to say that he cannot operate or function properly in society. I did not know the man and I know no more about him now. Maybe he had a job, and he went to this job every day as some people do, and he sat behind a desk or a counter and counted money and got his pay cheque every week and spent it all exactly one day before his next one came in, just like everyone else. The world isn't so different. Most people just do that sort of thing. They go to work and they make money, and they see some money flutter away from them before they even have it, which is called taxes, and then they go home and spend their money on silly things they don't really need.

Taxes are still being charged, but I don't know who collects them. I don't believe they are being spent. If there are politicians left, I suspect they are living off of the taxes as usual, but I would never go so far as to suggest that the taxes are being spent on the improvement of society. I find that taxes are generally collected more because they can be collected rather than because they are actually needed.

When I continued my journey westward, I knew already that I was now searching for the great Dr. Patricia R. Durham, but I had no idea of what I would find. It was a mystery to me. I just did not know what to expect. Neither did I realise that I was being watched.

There is a force more powerful than anything on Earth, and that force is called God, and God watches over everything. God can afford to because God has no limits to how many splits can be contained within one consciousness.

This is called Omniscience.

It is called Omnipotence.

It is called many things, and all of them eventually will mean GOD.

That is something everyone must learn: all things eventually will mean GOD. This does not mean that everything is God, or that everything will become God, or even that everything is a part of God.

It just means

that everything means

God.

This is a lesson I have learned. It is a lesson that I had to journey across the country to fully learn.

All in all, it is not an important lesson. It is not something that is required to live on this Earth. In that sense, it is not an important lesson. But in reality it is vital, and it would change everything on this planet. But most people aren't too concerned about that sort of thing any more. They just want to get by. They are happy watching television, avoiding work, eating bad food, and drinking, and paying bills. Everyone really just wants to *mind their own business* but that isn't something they can do. The last thing they want to worry about is other people. They just don't have the time or the money.

Time Is Money

Those are magic words of an ancient history that hardly anyone must remember now. I guess it must have been true, then, because that's what everyone says. But I don't think so.

I have also heard that *you can't take it with you*. This is true.

The problem that some people have is that they have not been convinced that what they are experiencing at any given moment is reality. Some people expect that what happens during one moment in fact is a mere prelude to what will really happen. That is why people who are in great danger, or who are in great fear, will often be heard saying to themselves: "This isn't happening. This isn't real."

Of course, it is happening, and it is real. But they will not believe that if someone tells them. They prefer to believe it is not real.

Some people think that way about everything that happens. They think the world itself is a prelude to what will really happen. I think now that most people think this way. They think the world has thrown them a curve, to throw them off track, but that as soon as they turn the corner, they will find reality waiting for them with big outstretched arms and a warm, motherly smile.

I would like to see it.

It would be better for a lot of people if they would stop expecting reality to show up late and accept that either everything is real or everything is not yet real, which is true. It is what a philosopher said once, although I don't recall which one. He said that there could not be two states of reality (or non-reality) within an either real or non-real world. He said everything was real, or else everything was not real. It was a question only of existence.

I believe it.

Yes, I had *things to do*. They were *important things to do*, and not one of them really mattered. That is something someone learns after one has walked across country without any real or tangible or clearly definable purpose because there just aren't really *important things to do*.

Some people will invent *important things to do* for themselves. Some people try to make as much money as they possible can, whether they need it all or not. I have also seen mathematicians sitting around a round circle puzzling over what X is and how it relates to Y and why there is no solution to , and they just don't realise how little it all really matters.

When I see things that I do not like, I rarely bother trying to make them into something more pleasing to me. Rarely is it worth making this attempt, because rarely will it change and rarely does it matter.

When persuasion fails, there is coercion. When coercion fails, there is destruction.

Magic words

for a magical world.

It is a pleasure to be left alone, to be generally unnoticed, to be at peace. This is not a general rule; it is an opinion and different people will disagree for different reasons. But other people agree.

One thing I have learned from life is that you should never care what other people say, and I live by that rule of thumb, or at least I try to. Some people feel their way through life by measuring and testing and groping and surveying the opinions and feelings of others. They have a social radar. They have faith in the popular belief. They believe in misconceptions if everyone else does.

But other people stumble and trip and knock themselves about through life without any regard for what other people say. These people are called true pioneers. They are the ones who make all the right mistakes, and they are laughed at, and ignored, and they are brilliant. They just do what they feel they have to do, even though everyone else says they are wrong. They do not listen to other people. They are not afraid. They are haphazard, and crazy, and to be avoided and admired at all costs.

I learned all of this only in retrospect. I know it now because I look back at these experiences in an effort to make sense of it all. I have learned a lot, and am not afraid to admit it.

One thing to do is to *mind your own business* and that will generally help you stay out of trouble. That is what I do now. It is what I have always tried to do. It is a safe bet, usually, if people will let you.

Chapter Thirty-One

The lunatic who had told me to travel west and find the great Dr. Patricia R. Durham was paying taxes. And he was living a crazy life at work and then he went outside every day and yelled at people, telling them whatever came to mind first, probably.

I knew that the great Dr. Patricia R. Durham had been living on the west coast for years, and legend has it that she has a great establishment there which is just about ready to take over the world, which I guess no one would really mind. Someone may as well take over, since no one seems to be in charge.

This assumes, of course, that someone needs to be in charge. So far it seems like no one really needs to be in charge. But I think if anyone can improve the human race, it's Dr. Patricia R. Durham, apprentice to the greatest genetic scientist in the universe. She doesn't need to be in charge to do that.

I know the man was crazy because I doubt so sincerely that the man could have sanely told me to go west knowing that I would find Dr. Patricia R. Durham there. Because most men are very frightened of her, and of any woman for that matter, and I don't think a sane one would tell me to go to the one woman who has it in her power to finally get rid of men indiscriminately, if she so chose to do this.

And this is true: she could do this. She can, I suspect, do anything she puts her mind to.

It is not by chance that she was my grandfather's assistant.

Seeing as she could do so much, and she was such a great scientist, it was pretty much taken for granted by everyone that she had all of the answers. She was a real know-it-all, and much revered or hated for that.

When I saw her, I was surprised at her frailty. See wore a turban upon her head, although I did not know why at the time. Hats are not popular now. They haven't been for as long as I can remember. But she wore one.

She was smoking when I came in, and she was smoking her eighth cigarette when I left.

I had seen her in a dream once. I hadn't realised then that she was the woman in this dream, but once I met her in real life, then I knew. I can say this honestly now: I met the great Dr. Patricia R. Durham

in real life. I think I am one of a very few people.

She lived in darkness and was pale. Her skin was very white. She had dark rings under her eyes. Maybe she never sleeps. Maybe somehow she had found late one night that even though she was

eternally exhausted, still she just could not sleep. I do not know if that is what happened, but maybe it is, in which case I would wonder when it happened.

She was very old. She was older than I'd imagined. But very beautiful.

When I arrived, she was sipping chamomile tea sweetened with honey, which she said she had gathered from her own bees. I believe her. Lots of people have spare time now. Enough time to raise bees. In their spare time, people often take on hobbies -- things they might not have tried before. Sometimes they are dangerous

hobbies, but rewarding as well, like bee farming.

We spoke for a few hours about who I might be, what I do in my spare time.

I did not mention who my grandfather had been. I decided that it would be best this way. We spoke about her own memories. Memories of the greatest scientist in the universe; my own grandfather.

Then she said that she remembered me, though I hadn't told her who I was. She couldn't tell me what my name was because her memory was getting too old to recall little details.

She also mentioned that sometimes she found that her mind could only remember the small details. She would see the small things in life, years and years ago. She would see a flower no one had gotten

for her in a decade. Or she would remember a name without placing the face.

Or an old story

Without the ending.

Generally speaking, I have a very good memory. It will probably get worse in my old age.

She did not know why I had come. She thought I'd come to interview her. She thought I was a member of the press and told me that she didn't give

interviews and that all comments were released through her press office, which is true as far as I know, because no one had so much as laid eyes upon her in years and all of her press releases were either

recordings of her voice only, or else just written out.

I told her that I was not a member of the press. I told her that I had come to meet her as an old friend.

This is when we began speaking of memories, both hazy and clear. And I listened, enraptured by the mere sound of the great woman's voice. Her words did not matter to me as much as the fact that she

was speaking. I do not remember now exactly what she was saying, in fact, but I know it was truth.

Someday, I will speak with such wisdom.

And at last, we had grown so close in just that one short half hour, she told me that she had to confess to me a terrible, neglected secret that she had been keeping. The only reason I reveal it here is that

by the time these, my memoirs, are read, both she and I will be but memories. We will be ghosts.

She said it was a strange secret because everyone knew it on some level, but no-one seemed aware of it.

I, of all people, should have known most of all.

She was not mutated.

Of course she wasn't. Anyone who knew about my grandfather, or of the great Dr. Patricia R. Durham's age, should realise that she was too old to be properly mutated. She was my mother's age at the time. To be mutated, she would have to be no older than me, since mutation is something that occurs before even the fetal stage of life.

She had hair

that the world had forgotten about. We'd all forgotten to notice, or to remember.

Her gray hair was beneath her turban. Her hair was woven together to keep it in place. It was strange,

but beautiful, on her.

She had a knife,

and she held it to my throat,

and held me close, and said that if I told anyone her age, or about my grandfather, or about her secret, then she would kill me. And I believed her.

The steel of the knife was cold against my flesh, and I could feel my sweat gather along the blade. I imagined it was blood, and I remember wondering why there was no pain.

She was like a mother to me in those few moments that she held me. I guess I could have killed her with just one glance, with the very gift she had given me and every living girl, but she wasn't afraid. I

have come to believe that this is her only vulnerability in the world.

But it did not frighten her.

She is, I imagine, afraid of nothing.

In those same moments, I was afraid nothing. I like to think that somehow we gave this to one another.

I do not know how.

When she'd put the knife away, she trembled, and wept. I did not understand then, and I still don't understand now. And this is what she said to me.

Chapter Thirty-One

"You don't understand."

She spoke these three words to me after I'd told her how Great she was, and how Brave, and how Wonderful it has been to turn the world around into a better place.

She just spoke in a trembling voice that I could barely hear.

And said no more.

When I left I was confused, because the things I now comprehend about our meeting was unknown to me at the time. I had not dreamed even in a nightmare that I would see the great Dr. Patricia R. Durham weep. And I had not dared dream of her holding me like a child she was about to send out into the world.

Once I caught a butterfly, and held it in my hands, cupped. And when at last I began feeling sorry for it, I opened my hands with my palms to the sky, and the butterfly spread its wings and flew away.

The air is magical.

There is no *private property* in the sky.

Every mutated baby girl is in some way a child of the great Dr. Patricia R. Durham's.

But when she held me in her arms

I was all of them.

And she released me so that I may flutter here and there in the sky, and never have to look at signs or be shot with salt guns or think about men, or hear people talk about the great Dr. Patricia R. Durham or my grandfather as if they were criminals.

She had sent forth a winged child,

and it was me,

and so I flew into the open air

and I don't believe I will ever come down.

Good-bye.

Or as I should say:

> Good-bye, and thank you very much for listening.
> > — Dr. Patricia R. Durham's traditional farewell, said at the end of her radio speeches

Credits

Story by Seth Kenlon

seth@straightedgelinux.com

Illustration of Modern Medusa is by Roxy at romawinkel.blogspot.com [http://romawinkel.blogspot.com]

Other elements from the Great Linux Multimedia Sprint. See slackermedia.info/downloads [http://slackermedia.info/downloads.html] for more information

Book, text, and audiobook are licensed cc-by-sa

See creativecommons.org/licenses/by-sa/3.0 [http://creativecommons.org/licenses/by-sa/3.0] for more information on Creative Commons, free culture, and copyleft licensing

The iconography in chapter 22 features public domain work from openclipart.org [http://www.openclipart.org] with works by molumen, nicubunu, TheresaKnott

Special thanks to SndChaser for the pdftk tip, Bill von Hagen for his dot-emacs file and xsltproc assistance, the Linux Kernel developers, Slackbook.org [http://slackbook.org], docbook.org [http://docbook.org], GNU, the FSF, KDE at large, perl, BASH, the Creative Commons, openclipart.org [http://openclipart.org], and everyone involved in and supportive of Free Software and free culture

Please also try experiencing this story in its audiobook form, available online at podiobooks.com [http://podiobooks.com]

Produced entirely using Free Software. See fsf.org [http://fsf.org] for more information.

BE SURE TO READ...

NOITULOVƎꓤ RADIO

the exciting upcoming sci fi novel from the
fantastic alternate universe-mind of Seth Kenlon!

After The Revolution.

Anarchy reins supreme, there are no laws. And it's *working*

People are building cities and living off the land and doing
whatever their passion prompts them to do. The land and its
resources are governed by a set of ancient documents known
only as the *GPL*, the *CC*, and *Berkley's Law*.

The Comm Techs.

They're called "commies" for short; they run all the
communication in the world, exclusively by radio and a device
known as the Konsole. The commies don't socialize much; they
just broadcast information, and monitor it, and archive it. It's a
regional system, and they're keeping it that way because global
communication is considered a thing of the "old world".

The New World.

One commie has a secret: she used to be a member of a
controversial revolutionary group dedicated to making sure
nothing from the Old World survived after the Revolution was
won. But now she's just a commie, up on her mountain Perch,
alone. She spends her days listening to broadcasts, archiving
information, and maintaining her radio tower.

And then one day, the daily broadcast doesn't come. Radio
silence. And it's up to her to go find out why.